High-Speed Showdown

As they drew nearer and the outlines of the boat became easier to make out, Joe became more and more sure that it was their quarry.

"That's Connie and Angelo," Joe announced, when they were about a hundred yards away. "But what are they up to?"

He could see that Connie was kneeling in the bottom of the boat, leaning way out over the side. Angelo was crouched next to her, with something long and narrow in his hands. As *Sleuth* drew nearer, he straightened up and glanced over his shoulder, then sprang to the controls. The engine must have been idling in neutral. Almost instantly, it sprang to life. The boat surged forward.

Then, just as Frank shoved *Sleuth*'s throttle all the way open, the motor on the rubber boat stalled. A passing wave turned it broadside, directly in the path of the Hardys' speedboat.

"Look out, Frank!" Joe shouted. "Turn! We're going to hit them!"

The Hardy Boys Mystery Stories

Available from MINSTREL Books

THE HARDY BOYS®

137

HIGH-SPEED SHOWDOWN

FRANKLIN W. DIXON

A MINSTREL® BOOK

Published by POCKET BOOKS
New York   London   Toronto   Sydney   Tokyo   Singapore

A MINSTREL PAPERBACK *Original*

A Minstrel Book published by
POCKET BOOKS, a division of Simon & Schuster Inc.
1230 Avenue of the Americas, New York, NY 10020

Copyright © 1996 by Simon & Schuster Inc.

Produced by Mega-Books, Inc.

ISBN: 0-671-50521-1

First Minstrel Books printing April 1996

10   9   8   7   6   5   4   3   2   1

THE HARDY BOYS MYSTERY STORIES is a trademark
of Simon & Schuster Inc.

THE HARDY BOYS, A MINSTREL BOOK and colophon
are registered trademarks of Simon & Schuster Inc.

Printed in the U.S.A.

Contents

HIGH-SPEED SHOWDOWN

1 Boats Ahoy!

Seventeen-year-old Joe Hardy turned into the driveway of the Hardy house and stopped the van a few feet from the garage door. After shutting off the engine, he climbed out, stretched to his full height of six feet, and brushed back a lock of blond hair from his eyes. Then he turned around and reached inside for the shopping bag on the passenger seat.

Suddenly something poked him in the back, just above the right kidney, and Joe stiffened. A voice growled, "Don't move!"

Instantly Joe flung himself backward and spun to the left. His left forearm swept upward, knocking his attacker's arm away from him. Then he made a grab with his right hand, trapping his

1

attacker's wrist. He was about to jerk the arm down across his thigh when he recognized his brother, Frank.

"Okay, okay!" Frank said with a grin. "If that's the way you feel about it, go ahead and move! But don't go far. We've got a date down at the Bayport Marina."

"Now?" Joe protested. "Aw, c'mon—I just bought a new set of wheels for my in-line skates. I was planning to mount them this morning, then try them out."

Frank shook his head. "It'll have to wait. Dad just called from San Diego. There's a case he wants us to look into for him."

Fenton Hardy, Joe and Frank's father, was a former New York City cop who now had a nation-wide reputation as a private investigator.

Joe was just about to ask what kind of case it was when Frank continued. "Didn't you say something the other day about wanting to go to the power-boat races this weekend?"

"Sure," Joe said, nodding. "It's the Northeast Nationals. Some of the fastest, most powerful offshore racing boats in the world are coming to Bayport."

"Then let's go. It looks like you're going to get your wish," Frank told him. "Dad had a call from a guy named Gerald Magnusson. He's a big real estate operator in Cleveland who's in charge of this year's race. He wanted Dad to help him."

Joe got behind the wheel, while Frank circled the van and climbed into the passenger seat.

"I get it," Joe said, restarting the engine. "Dad told him he's busy. But he just happened to know of two brilliant young detectives in Bayport who just happen to be available. Right?"

"Something like that," Frank agreed. "Anyway, right after I got off the phone with Dad, Magnusson called. Apparently, somebody's out to sabotage the races. He asked us to come over right away. He sounded pretty worried. He's at race headquarters, at the Waterside Inn."

"Well, what are we waiting for?" Joe demanded. He backed out of the driveway and started across Bayport, in the direction of the harbor. As he turned onto Shore Road, he glanced over at Frank and asked, "Did this guy Magnusson tell you who he thinks is behind the sabotage?"

Frank shook his head. "Nope. He said he'd give us the details when he sees us. I got the feeling—"

"Hey, will you look at that!" Joe exclaimed, interrupting him.

A big eighteen-wheeler had just turned onto the street ahead of them. Strapped to its flatbed trailer was a sleek V-hulled powerboat. The words *Blue Flame* were painted on the side in curvy metallic silver letters.

Frank whistled. "Will you look at the size of that baby . . . it must be forty feet long! Next to

3

that, the *Sleuth* would look like a bathtub toy."
Sleuth was the Hardys' outboard runabout.

Joe grinned. "Yeah, but at least we have room to take a few friends out on the water. You take that monster . . . I bet it seats four people, max. All the rest of it is full of machinery—two or even three big supercharged V-8 engines."

"How fast will a boat like that go?" Frank asked, curious.

Joe shrugged. "I'm not sure," he admitted. "A hundred miles an hour, at least. Maybe a lot more, in calm water. Hey, what—"

The truck had just crossed Wright Street and started down the slope that led to the harbor. Its brake lights flashed brightly, but it looked to Joe as if the big vehicle was picking up speed instead of slowing down. Suddenly the blare of its horn split the air. The trailer and its high-tech cargo started to sway from side to side.

"The driver's losing control," Frank said. He leaned forward and gripped the edge of the dashboard. "Is there anything we can do to help?"

Joe was concentrating on keeping a margin of safety between the van and the runaway truck. He shook his head and said, "I don't see how. If he's lost his brakes, I just hope he's a good swimmer. There's nothing big enough to stop him between here and the harbor."

After a moment Joe added, "No, I think it's

4

okay. He's slowing down. Whatever the problem was, it looks like it's under control."

"Just in time, too," Frank pointed out as the eighteen-wheeler came to a stop at the corner of Shore Road and Water Street. "Pull over, Joe. I'd like to do a little nosing around. This may sound crazy, but if somebody's playing dirty tricks on the racers, maybe we just saw one of them."

Joe pulled into the nearest vacant spot. As he set the parking brake, he asked, "Do you really think there's something suspicious about what just happened?"

"Not necessarily," Frank replied, pushing his door open. "Trucks do lose control on hills. But I wouldn't mind knowing more about why it happened this time."

Across the street, the driver of the truck had climbed down from the cab and was stooping over to check the hoses that connected the brake systems of the tractor and trailer. Joe watched Frank go over to him and start talking. The driver straightened up, pointed at the hill, then waved one hand in a gesture that said, "Who knows!" Then he turned his back on Frank and walked away. The conversation was over.

Joe got out and locked the van. Frank waited for a gap in the traffic, then sprinted across to join him.

"Nothing wrong with the truck," Frank reported. "The guy just isn't much of a driver. Pretty lucky, though. He could have easily ended up in the drink."

"Him, and a quarter million dollars' worth of racing boat," Joe added. "And the way it's strapped to the trailer, I doubt if it would float."

As he and Frank started up Water Street, Joe noticed that the Bayport Marina parking lot had been turned into a sort of fairgrounds. The tents and trailers of exhibitors were lined up in long rows. Mingled aromas of hot dogs, Italian sausages, and shish kebab wafted across the street, making Joe's stomach growl. Would their meeting with Magnusson leave enough time for a prelunch snack?

The Waterside Inn had been an important town landmark since the days when Bayport's fleet of whaling ships prowled the world's oceans in search of prey. The central section of the inn was white with green shutters and had a wide covered veranda across the front. It still looked a lot like the old photos that were on display in the Bayport Library. But in recent years it had sprouted two wings that looked more like a budget motel than a quaint seaside inn.

The sidewalk was crowded. As Joe and Frank neared the stairs that led up to the inn, a girl of about sixteen caught Joe's eye and took a step forward. She had brown eyes, a freckled nose, and long brown hair pulled back in a ponytail. Her T-shirt showed a whale, a dolphin, and a seal, with the words *Save the Ocean* over them.

"Hi," the girl said with a smile. "You guys go to Bayport High, don't you? I think I've seen you around."

"That's right," Frank said. "I'm Frank Hardy, and this is my brother, Joe."

"Oh, yeah, I've heard about you. I'm Connie Fernandez," the girl replied. "I'm a sophomore."

Joe recognized her name. "You were part of that environmental slate for student government, weren't you? How'd you do?"

"I won," she said simply. "It's a great start, but there's still lots of work to be done. Listen—are you fellows here for the boat races? Because if you are, I'd like you to take a look at this."

She dug into a big manila envelope that said Earthquest on it and took out a leaflet. As she handed it to Frank, Joe could read the words across the top: The Ocean Is a Home, NOT a Racetrack!

Connie reached over and grabbed Joe's arm. "How do you think you'd feel if a bunch of people came roaring through your house at ninety miles an hour, stinking it up with exhaust fumes and scaring you half to death?" she demanded.

"Pretty mad," Joe admitted dryly. "But I'm not a fish."

7

"That doesn't matter, Joe," Connie told him. "Some marine mammals are every bit as smart and sensitive as we are. Don't they have a right to be left alone? And that's not all. Do you have any idea what humongous gas guzzlers these racing boats are, and how much exhaust and pollution they pour into the ocean? It's a crime to waste our natural resources on something so stupid and pointless."

Joe scratched his head. He thought it was neat the way Connie stood up for her ideas, and he was for saving the whales as much as anybody. On the other hand, he was really looking forward to watching the big boats in action. Whether Connie liked it or not, speed and power were exciting.

Frank said, "Connie, I'd really like to hear more of what you've got to say, but we're late for an appointment. Will you be around this afternoon?"

"Sure, if my supply of leaflets holds out," she replied. "I just got these from the printer yesterday, but they're going fast. If they don't last, I'll have to go run off some more. It's important to make people think about what they're doing."

"Catch you later," Joe said over his shoulder as he and Frank started up the steps to the inn. He noticed Frank carefully fold Connie's leaflet and put it in the back pocket of his jeans.

The management of the inn had set tables and chairs out on the front porch. Every place was taken. Those who hadn't managed to grab a seat milled around, going from table to table, pausing to say hello to acquaintances. A number of people were wearing bright red, white, and blue jackets with *Offshore Racing* embroidered in fancy script letters on the back.

As Joe and Frank were crossing the porch, one of the jacket wearers took a step backward and stumbled into Joe. He was about seventeen, with blond hair and the deep tan of someone who spent a lot of time outdoors.

"Oh, sorry," he said quickly, with a twinkle in his blue eyes. "I should watch where I'm going."

"No problem," Joe said. He noticed the name on the guy's badge—Dave Hayman—and added, "Hey, I recognize your name. Didn't you win a couple of big junior titles last year?"

Dave's face lit with pleasure. "My brother and I did, yeah. I don't know you, do I? Are you racing this weekend?"

"Nope, just a fan," Joe replied. He introduced himself and Frank, then asked, "What's the name of your boat? We'll root for you."

Dave made a face. "Unfortunately, I'm going to be in the rooting section, too," he said. "The man who sponsored us—his company is having a bad year, and that makes it a *terrible* year for us. No sponsor, no boat. No boat, no racing."

"That's really rough," Frank said.

"Yeah." Dave sighed. "It won't be easy, just standing on the shore and watching, when I could

9

be out there at the controls of a boat," he admitted. "Still, it's better—"

Behind him, the wide front door of the inn flew open and crashed against the wall. Two men came storming out onto the porch. The first was about forty-five, of medium height, with dark hair, powerful shoulders, and a scowling face. The other man was taller and younger, about thirty, with long brown hair, a square jaw, and the build of a gymnast. He was wearing a heavy gold chain with what looked like a carved ivory medallion hanging from it. Joe thought he looked familiar but couldn't place him.

"Hold it, Newcastle," the younger man called. He grabbed the other man's shoulder and tried to spin him around. "I haven't finished saying what I've got to say to you."

Newcastle turned and brushed the hand from his shoulder, growling, "Too bad, because I've finished listening, Batten. I'm sick of you *and* that cute plastic necklace of yours."

He reached out, as if to flick the ivory medallion with his forefinger. Batten took a step back, then cocked his fist to throw a punch. The people sitting at tables nearby scrambled for safety, and several chairs were knocked over.

Joe decided that the two men had to be stopped before someone got hurt. He caught Frank's eye and gestured with his head toward Newcastle.

10

Then, as Frank moved toward the older man, Joe stepped in front of Batten.

"Hey, pal," he said in a soothing voice. "Let's all take it easy, okay?"

Batten's face contorted. "Sure, *pal!*" he said through clenched teeth. As he aimed a fast blow at Joe's midsection, he added, "Try taking *this* easy!"

2 Threats and Menaces

The instant Joe saw the fist rocketing toward his stomach, his hundreds of hours of training and practice in the martial arts took over. Smoothly, seemingly without thought or effort, he swayed to the left and twisted his body sideways from the hips.

The movement was just enough to allow Batten's blow to slip harmlessly past him. As it did, Joe grasped Batten's wrist in his right hand and put his left hand behind the other man's elbow. To a spectator, it might have looked as innocent as the grip Joe would have used to help an elderly person across the street. But Batten went spinning across the porch, hit the white wooden railing, and did a back flip over it into the hedge.

12

Several onlookers hurried over to help Batten out of the bushes. Joe stayed where he was. He figured that if he tried to help, he would simply rouse Batten's temper again. He glanced around. Frank was standing with one hand on the shoulder of the man Batten had been arguing with. The man looked at Frank and shrugged, as if to say that the quarrel hadn't been his fault.

From the door of the inn, a voice full of authority demanded, "What's going on out here?" The speaker was a man of about sixty, with thick gray hair and a white mustache. He was wearing white slacks, a blue blazer, a white button-down shirt, and a regimental striped tie. Joe noticed that his white deck shoes were spotless.

The man next to Frank stepped forward and said, "It's nothing, Gerald. Barry and I had words, that's all. Then, when these two kids tried to smooth things over, Barry got physical." He chuckled and added, "As you can see, it didn't quite work out the way he expected."

"Carl, I'm surprised at Barry *and* you," the man replied. "Surprised, and very disappointed. The idea of a national champion and a leading contender for the title scrapping like a couple of fourth-grade schoolyard toughs! And in public, too. Is that the kind of image we want people to have of powerboat racing?"

"Guess not," Carl Newcastle said, with a little shrug. He didn't sound very convinced. "Sorry."

13

"Well, *I'm* not sorry," Barry called from the foot of the steps. "I don't need you to teach me how to act, Gerald. What this sport really needs is more colorful personalities that attract the public, not more fuddy-duddy rules. As for you, Newcastle, I'll settle with you on the water, on Saturday."

Barry turned to go, but not before he gave Joe a dirty look.

"Congratulations, brother. You really know how to win new friends," Frank murmured.

Before Joe could think of a comeback, the man in the blue blazer said, "Am I right in thinking that you two are Fenton Hardy's boys? I'm Gerald Magnusson."

Frank and Joe introduced themselves and shook hands with Magnusson. Then he led them indoors. As they followed him, Joe told Frank, "That turkey who tried to deck me? That must be Barry Batten. He won the national offshore title last year."

"Oh, right," Frank replied. "I remember seeing an interview with him on TV. He said he owed all his victories to his lucky medallion. It's a piece of whale ivory that was carved by some ancestor of his who was captain of a whaling ship."

Magnusson took them to a small room off the lobby that was set up as an office.

"Thank you for coming by," he said, after they all sat down. "I apologize for the greeting you just got. I'm afraid everyone's nerves are on edge."

14

"Why's that, sir?" Frank asked.

Magnusson stroked his mustache with one forefinger. "It's hard to explain," he said slowly. "In the last two days, since the racers have started arriving in Bayport, there have been several, ah, incidents. Nothing terribly startling, really—equipment breaking down when it shouldn't, that sort of thing. But the rumor has spread that someone is out to wreck the meet. I wanted your father—and since he's not available, of course, you—to find out if there's any truth to the rumor."

"I see," Frank said.

"I've been part of the offshore racing scene for many years," Magnusson continued. "But this is the first time I've had responsibility for a major meet. I don't want anything to go wrong."

"We understand," Joe told him. "But what kind of incidents are you talking about?"

Magnusson frowned. "Well, for one thing . . . tell me what you think of this."

He took a sheet of paper from his desktop and handed it to the Hardys. Joe peered over Frank's shoulder and caught his breath. It looked like the leaflet they had seen Connie distributing earlier, but with an important difference. At the bottom, the words *Polluters Die* were scrawled under a crude skull and crossbones.

"How did you get this?" Frank asked.

"It arrived by fax about an hour ago,"

Magnusson told him. "Somebody's idea of a joke, obviously."

"Not a very funny one," Joe pointed out. "Especially if somebody ends up getting hurt."

Magnusson stood up and crossed to the window. With his back to them, he said, "You agree that I should take it seriously, then."

"I think *we* should take it seriously," Frank said. "Listen, sir, what do you think of this? We'll look into it, very quietly. If it does turn out to be a bad joke, fine. And if not, we'll have a better idea of what you're facing and what to do about it. Do you have a photocopier here? I'd like a copy of this."

"Why, yes," Magnusson said, sounding surprised. He took the leaflet and stepped outside. A few moments later, he returned with a photocopy and gave it to Frank.

"I'd rather people don't know you've been hired to investigate," Magnusson said. "It'll only stir things up even more if they know. Is that okay with you?"

"We prefer working undercover," Frank said.

"I'm sure you're very good at it," Magnusson replied. "Here, I'll make out passes for you."

He took two tags marked Staff and wrote in their names, then signed them. As he handed them over, he smiled and said, "If anyone asks, just say your dad and I are old friends. My position does carry a few privileges with it, along with far too

16

many headaches. Now, why don't I take you down to the dock and introduce you to a few people?"

The crowds on Water Street were thicker now. Most of the people were strolling in the direction of the exposition. Lots of them paused along the way to stare through the fence at the docked racing boats. Frank and Joe showed their new passes to the guard at the gate and followed Magnusson out onto the main pier.

"You can't imagine what a complex business it is, organizing a meet like this," Magnusson remarked, as they walked out between the two lines of slips. "We've got almost a hundred entries, broken down into ten different classes. Most of our spectators come out to watch the really big, really fast Open Class boats. But the racers in the A, B, and C classes are every bit as important to the sport. Every bit as exciting, too, in my opinion."

"How does it work?" Frank asked. "Do all the boats race at the same time?"

Magnusson shook his head. "No. You do see that at smaller, one-day meets. But with an event of this size, it would be too dangerous and confusing. For each class we'll run a series of heats over the next couple of days. Then on Saturday, there'll be the final of each class. The top boats will have a shot at winning prizes and championship points."

"Prizes?" Joe repeated. "You mean, money?"

"The grand prize winner of the super boats this

17

year will take home a silver trophy and a check for one hundred thousand dollars," Magnusson replied. "Of course, almost all of the others will just be taking home their memories."

And some very hefty bills to pay, Frank thought to himself, as he looked over the sleek, powerful boats on either side of him.

Joe touched Frank on the arm and said in a low voice, "Look—isn't that what's-her-name, who plays the lead on *Brisbane Lane?*"

Frank looked. About twenty feet down the dock was a tall, slim young woman in tight blue biking shorts and a bright yellow crop top that set off her mane of tawny blond hair. She was talking to a guy of about thirty-five, with longish black hair and a neatly trimmed black beard. He was wearing very faded jeans and a Baja California T-shirt. Judging by their gestures, Frank didn't think the two were having a friendly conversation.

"If it isn't her, it's her twin sister," he told Joe. "Susan Shire, right?"

Magnusson cut in. "That's right," he said. "And that's Dennis Shire she's talking to. Her ex-husband. He owns a software company. They're both real enthusiasts about offshore racing. They were a terrific team when they were still together. Now they're more like not-so-friendly rivals. Here, let me introduce you."

As they drew nearer, Frank heard Dennis say, "You wouldn't know anything about somebody

18

fouling up the timing of my fuel injection system, would you?"

"Sure I would," Susan replied. Frank could hear the sarcasm in her voice. "You can't lift the hatch on an engine compartment without fouling up something. That's why, in the old days, I'd handle all our tune-ups. Remember?"

Frank wasn't sure if he should back away from this family quarrel or pay particularly close attention. These two were important competitors, after all.

"Ha!" Dennis said. "That was just to help you feel important. You'd better believe that I always checked everything out afterward."

"Susan, Dennis," Magnusson said. "May I—"

"In a minute," Susan said, without looking around. "'Feel important'? You pig! Have you happened to notice who's been winning races since I had the good sense to dump you? And I'm going to take the cup this weekend, too, don't worry."

Dennis said, "Worry? Fat chance! I've got nothing to worry about if you're the competition. And the only hope you have to win is if you mess up my boat. And don't *you* worry, I'm going to be on the lookout for that."

"Well, look out for this!" With a sudden movement, Susan put both hands on Dennis's chest and shoved. Taken by surprise, he stumbled backward a few steps. His ankle caught on the mooring line of the nearest boat. Off balance, he fell back over the edge of the dock. His arms flailed as he tried to grab something to break his fall. Frank heard a distinct thump as the back of the man's head slammed against the pointed bow of the boat.

As Frank watched openmouthed, Dennis tumbled limply into the oil-slicked water of the boat slip. Bubbles rose to the surface as he began to sink out of sight.

3 Just the Fax, Ma'am

"Dennis!" Susan cried, clapping her hands to the sides of her face. "Oh, no! What have I done? Somebody, please, *help!*"

Frank had already ripped off his T-shirt and was yanking at the laces of his running shoes. Next to him, Joe was doing the same.

"No! I'll go in after him," Frank said quickly. "You get ready to pull us out."

Not waiting for Joe to reply, Frank slipped out of his shoes and ran to the edge of the dock. He made a lightning-quick judgment of distances, then jumped. He landed in the water less than a yard from Dennis, who was obviously still dazed by the blow to his head. He'd slipped just below the surface, and his eyes had rolled upward.

21

Two powerful overhand strokes took Frank to his side. He hooked his elbow under the drowning man's chin and took a quick glance around. Joe was lying flat on the dock half a dozen feet away, reaching out his hands to help. Frank rolled onto his back and used the frog kick to make his way toward Joe. A few more powerful kicks got him and Dennis close to the dock.

"Okay, Frank, I've got him," Joe said.

"Great," Frank replied as he felt Dennis's weight being lifted from him. "Watch his head. One bump like that is more than enough."

Frank swam out of the way and saw that Joe wasn't alone. Dave Hayman, the young blond guy they'd met a little earlier, was helping lift Dennis onto the dock. A moment later Frank heard Dennis cough loudly, then gasp, "It's okay, I'm all right. Just give me a second to catch my breath."

Relieved, Frank glanced around. He could have hoisted himself directly onto the dock, but he knew better than to try it. He really didn't want to go home with a crop of ferocious splinters. On the other side of the slip, a wooden ladder extended down into the water. He started swimming toward it, which wasn't easy with sodden jeans clinging to his legs.

Gerald Magnusson was waiting at the head of the ladder. "Well done, Frank," he said, offering his hand. "Would you like me to find you some dry clothes?"

22

"Thanks, I'm okay," Frank replied. He picked his T-shirt up off the dock and pulled it on over his head, then slipped his feet into his shoes. He felt incredibly grungy after his plunge in the harbor. All he wanted at the moment was to go home to take a long, hot shower.

Frank saw that Dennis was on his feet, though he kept one hand on Dave's shoulder for support. Susan, still pale, hurried over to him.

"Oh, Dennis, darling," she cried. "Are you sure you're all right? I can't believe that happened."

Joe looked over at Frank and rolled his eyes. Had Susan forgotten that she was the one who'd shoved her ex-husband into the water?

"Oh, it happened, all right," Dennis replied grimly. "Too bad these fellows rescued me. Your trial would have put your photo on page one of every supermarket tabloid in America."

Susan's face hardened. "That's not very funny, Dennis," she declared. "You know very well that I didn't mean—"

Dennis cut in. "To murder me? No, I suppose not. Not in front of all these witnesses, anyway. But I'd better remember to stay out of dark alleys."

Susan glared at him, then glared at Dave, as well, who was still supporting Dennis. Frank saw Dave redden and look down at his feet. He must be wondering what he'd gotten into, and how to get out of it.

23

Susan turned abruptly and marched away.

"That wasn't a very fair accusation, Dennis," Magnusson said.

Dennis's shoulders slumped. "No, I guess not," he said. He reached up and brushed a lock of damp black hair off his forehead. "I'll have to apologize . . . but not just yet."

He turned to Frank and said, "I owe you one, buddy, you and your friends. I know Dave here, but we haven't met, have we?"

Magnusson stepped in and introduced Joe and Frank, adding, "They're eager to find out more about offshore racing. If you have a little time to give them . . ."

"You bet," Dennis said. "Tell you what—are you guys free around two this afternoon? I'm taking *Adelita* out for a practice run. How'd you like to come along for the ride?"

"That'd be great," Frank said in the same moment that Joe said, "Terrific."

"Okay, it's a date," Dennis said with a grin. "Two o'clock, slip B-forty-eight. Now, I'd better go get into some dry clothes. Wouldn't it be awful to blow the big race because I caught a cold?"

"And I'd better get back to my duties," Magnusson said. "Frank, Joe, stop by to see me later, if you have a moment."

"We'll do that," Frank promised.

As soon as Dennis and Magnusson walked away, Dave turned to Frank and Joe and asked, "Hey,

24

just what went down here? I didn't want to ask before."

"Dennis accused his ex-wife, Susan, of tampering with his boat engine," Frank explained. "Then she got mad and pushed him, and he tripped and fell in. That's the second shoving match we've seen since we got here. Are these boat races usually so lively?"

Dave wrinkled his forehead. "Not at all," he replied. "People do their best to win, sure. That's what races are about. But once it's over with, everybody's usually real buddy-buddy. After all, it's a pretty small circle, offshore racing. Everybody knows everybody, even though we come from all over the map. These meets are our big chance to see each other. No, there's definitely something weird going on around here."

"Any idea what exactly?" Joe asked.

"Just a mood," Dave said with a shake of his head. "I can't really say more than that."

"Well, if you hear anything, will you pass it along to us?" Frank asked. When Dave gave him a curious look, he said, "We don't want our guests to go home with a bad impression of Bayport."

Judging from his expression, Frank could tell that Dave still thought he was a bit off the wall. But Dave nodded and said, "Sure. What are you guys up to now?"

"I'd better go home and change," Frank said. "But we'll come right back. And we'll keep an eye out for you. This is all new to us, so I'm sure we're going to have a lot of questions."

Dave laughed. "Well, I hope I have a few answers, then. Okay, catch you later." He turned and walked slowly out along the dock, studying the boats on either side as he went.

Frank watched him for a few moments, then said, "It must be rough for him, coming to a race like this and not being able to take part in it. Come on, let's head for home. I don't mind wet jeans so much, but wet, *oily* jeans . . ."

Joe was glancing through the mail when Frank came downstairs after showering and changing. Frank headed straight for the computer and reached for a boxed set of CD-ROMs. Joe recognized it. He and Frank had bought it only a couple of weeks earlier. It was supposed to contain every telephone directory in the entire United States. So far, they hadn't had a chance to test it.

"What are you doing?" Joe asked. "Trying to look up some girl you used to know?"

"This is strictly business," Frank replied. "The instructions claim we can use this gadget as a reverse directory."

"Meaning?"

"You input a telephone number, and it tells you who it belongs to," Frank explained. "*If* it's listed, of course. You can even search by a particular address, if you want."

26

Joe's eyes widened. "So if we have a number," he said, "we can find out not only whose it is, but we can find out who his neighbors are? This is a little scary, Frank."

Frank grinned. "It's the information revolution in action," he replied. "And as usual, the hardest part will be figuring out how to make it work. Here, why don't you look over the so-called 'Quick and E-Z User's Guide.'"

After a few minutes of study, Joe said, "I've worked out how to look up motels in Montana. Will that help?"

"Only if that leaflet came from there," Frank said.

"And how do we find that out?" Joe demanded.

Frank showed him the copy of the threatening leaflet Magnusson had received by fax that morning. "You see that tiny line of type at the top?" he said. "Part of it's the number of the fax machine that sent it. It's in our area code, so I'm trying to put a name and address to it. Let's see what happens if I click on that bell icon."

"Hey, okay!" Joe exclaimed, peering at the monitor screen over Frank's shoulder. "Try typing in the number."

Frank's fingers flew. After a tiny pause, the screen rewrote itself. Frank sat back, grinning. "There we go," he announced. "That fax came from Pinkham's Pharmacy, in the 1700 block of

27

Calhoun Street. Let's go find out what Mr. or Ms. Pinkham can tell us about this."

As Frank pushed his chair back from the table, Aunt Gertrude appeared in the doorway.

"Not so fast," she said. "You boys aren't going anywhere until I've seen you eat a good lunch. There are chicken sandwiches with my special peach chutney all ready for you."

Frank and Joe exchanged a look. They knew better than to cross Aunt Gertrude when she was set on feeding them. She was perfectly capable of hiding the keys to the van to keep them home.

"Uh . . . thanks, Aunt Gertrude," Joe said.

"That sounds great," Frank added. As the words left his mouth, he realized that he meant them.

Twenty minutes later, comfortably full, the Hardys were on their way. Calhoun Street was just half a mile or so from the marina. They parked in front of Pinkham's Pharmacy and went inside. From behind the counter, a middle-aged man in a white jacket looked up and said, "May I help you?"

Frank glanced at his name badge. "I hope so, Mr. Pinkham," he said with a smile, and showed him the leaflet. "We're trying to find out who sent us this. He forgot to put his name on it."

Pinkham put on his glasses and peered at the leaflet, then shook his head. "Sorry," he said.

"It was sent from here, wasn't it?" Joe asked.

"Oh, yes, right after I opened this morning," the druggist replied. "But I can't tell you who sent it. I found it on the floor under the mail slot, with a couple of dollar bills clipped to it. There was a note that gave the number to fax it to. I thought it was a little odd, to tell you the truth, but I didn't see the harm in sending it. It was already paid for, after all."

At Frank's request, he found the original of the leaflet and the note with Magnusson's number. The Hardys studied them, but nothing seemed to point to the sender's identity.

They were about to leave when Frank had a thought. "What time did you open this morning?"

"Nine," the druggist told him. "But I'm always here by quarter of."

As they drove toward the Waterside Inn, Frank said, "So the leaflet had to be put in the mail slot before eight forty-five this morning. I wonder when Connie started passing them out."

"Not that early, I bet," Joe said. "You think she . . ."

"We'll ask her," Frank replied.

They found Connie in front of the inn, handing out leaflets. This time she had a helper, a stocky guy with dark hair and thick black eyebrows.

"Hi, Frank, Joe," Connie called when she saw the Hardys. "You guys know Angelo Losordo?"

Joe nodded. "We were in Ms. Vigotsky's history class together. How's it going, Angelo?"

"Okay so far," Angelo said, with a hint of distrust in his voice.

Frank took the fax from his pocket and said, "Connie, will you look at this?"

She glanced at it, then shrugged. "So?"

"Do you know anything about it?" Joe asked.

"Sure. It looks like one of our leaflets that somebody scribbled on," she replied. "So what?

"Somebody faxed it to the meet office," Frank replied. " 'Polluters die.' Doesn't that sound like a threat to you?"

"Not necessarily. Maybe it just means that pollution kills. Which it does. Anyway, we've got nothing to do with this," Connie insisted. "We don't have to fax those guys anything. We're right out here *telling* them what we have to say."

As if to prove her point, she turned and offered a leaflet to an approaching pedestrian, a guy with brown hair. He took it, crumpled it up, and threw it on the sidewalk.

"Hey, mister," Angelo said. "That's called littering, and it's against the law."

"That's where this garbage belongs," the man growled.

Frank recognized him. Barry Batten, the guy with the medallion whom Joe had tangled with earlier. Batten obviously recognized Joe, too. He clenched his fists as if getting ready for a rematch.

"I should have known you were one of these eco-kooks," he said to Joe.

Connie stepped between them. Staring pointedly at Batten's medallion, she said, "We know about you, too." Joe noticed she was purposely projecting her voice to attract attention. "And if you think it'll bring you good luck to wear jewelry made from a murdered whale, you are simply too gross to live."

"Don't you threaten me!" Batten roared.

"I don't have to," Connie replied, just as loudly. She looked around at the gathering crowd, then added, "As for your precious boat race, forget it. You might as well go home now. I'm going to make sure it'll never happen."

4 The Tension Mounts

Frank saw a look of rage take over Barry Batten's face. He raised his right hand over his left shoulder, as if he was about to give her a backhanded slap across the face. Out of the corner of his eye, Frank saw Connie's coworker, Angelo, drop into a tense crouch, preparing to jump Barry. In another moment, the argument was going to turn into an open brawl.

"Hold it," Frank said, in a low but commanding voice. He put his arm out horizontally, blocking Angelo. "Joe, take Connie somewhere quiet where you can talk."

"Frank Hardy, if you think you can order *me*—" Connie began.

"Butt out, pal," Barry said, overriding her. "I can handle her kind anytime."

Frank wanted to roll his eyes in frustration. That's what happened when you tried to separate two angry people—more often than not, they both decided to turn on you.

Dave Hayman appeared. Even though he was half Barry's age, he looked just as disgusted as Frank was by the childish behavior of his fellow racer. "Come on, Barry," he urged, taking his arm. "All you're doing is giving these people the attention they want. Get into a fight with them, and you'll watch them being interviewed on the evening news, spouting all that stuff about how boat racing is bad for the environment. Is that what you want?"

Barry hesitated. "Well . . ."

Dave lowered his voice, but Frank caught the word "champion." Whatever Dave said, it worked. After glaring once more at Connie, Angelo, and Joe, Barry turned away and walked up the path toward the inn. Dave caught Frank's eye and gave an almost unnoticeable wink, then followed Barry.

"The nerve of that dude," Angelo said, from behind Frank. "Why'd you stop me from decking him?"

"I'm glad he did," Connie said before Frank could reply. "That would have been horrible for

33

our image. The whole purpose of Earthquest is to make people more responsible citizens of the natural world. We're not going to do that by starting fistfights."

"Sometimes you can't do one without the other," Angelo said sullenly. "Do you really think you can reason with somebody like Batten?"

"I know we have to try," Connie told him. "And if he *won't* listen to reason, we'll make sure people know it."

Frank was very interested by this glimpse of Connie's strategy—or at least of what she wanted people like him and Joe to believe was her strategy. He made a mental note to find time for a longer talk with her. Right now, however, he was more concerned with the faxed threat. Could that, too, be part of Connie's strategy? To disrupt the boat races in the name of the environment?

"You wrote this leaflet especially for the power-boat meet, didn't you?" he said, in what he hoped was a casual voice.

Connie frowned. "Well, sure. Why?"

"How long have you been giving them to people? Was today the first day?" Frank continued.

"Hey, what is this?" Connie demanded. Her frown deepened.

"It's a simple question," Joe said. "Why not answer it?"

Angelo stepped forward, with his chin jutting

34

out. "Watch it, Connie," he said. "These guys are up to something. I've heard rumors around school that they're amateur detectives or something. I think they're trying to pin something on us."

Connie gave Frank a narrow-eyed look. "It's that leaflet you showed me before, isn't it? You're trying to make out that *I* sent it. Well, I already told you I didn't, and that's the last word I'm going to say about it. Now you'll have to excuse us— we've got important work to do."

Head high, she walked right past Frank and Joe and went back to handing leaflets to people in the crowd. After dividing a dirty look equally between the two Hardys, Angelo followed her.

"There go my chances of winning the 'Most Popular' title," Joe muttered. "What now?"

Frank glanced at his watch. "We've got half an hour before our ride with Dennis," he observed. "Why don't we check out some of the exhibits? I'd like to get more of a feel for what's happening."

They crossed the street to the fairgrounds and started down the first of the rows. The booths were a strange mixture. All sorts of food was available, from fried potato curls and Pennsylvania Dutch funnel cakes to Middle Eastern pastries and Oriental spring rolls. Frank was sure he had seen some of the same booths at the Founders Day street fair a few weeks earlier.

Some of the merchandise booths looked very

35

familiar, too. There were racks of CDs and video-cassettes, and piles of unlabeled T-shirts and jeans supposedly from a famous nationwide chain. In front of one tiny booth, a man was demonstrating a miracle sponge mop. He kept talking nonstop, even though none of the passersby paused to listen.

Other booths, however, had a real nautical flavor. One was selling bright yellow raingear that looked able to keep out the fiercest North Atlantic storm. At another, earnest fairgoers were peering at finely machined propellers and asking detailed questions of the two people behind the table. There was also a booth that featured a speedboat of about eighteen feet. Even strapped to a trailer, Joe thought its sleek lines and huge outboard motor made it look ready for an incredible day of cruising and waterskiing.

"Frank, look at this," Joe said, dragging him toward a table of rugged-looking electronic gear. "Would you believe a handheld GPS receiver!"

"Great," Frank replied, gazing down at a gadget that looked something like a cross between a personal TV and a cellular phone. "Is that anything like a wide receiver? Or a tailback?"

Joe gave him a disgusted look. "Ha, ha," he said. "Don't you know what that little package can do? It'll tell you where you are, anywhere on earth. Just push a button, and you can read out your exact latitude and longitude, within a few

36

dozen yards. It works off signals from satellites. I think we ought to have one for the van. Can you imagine how great that would be if we ever got lost?"

Frank gave a snort. "With what that gizmo must cost, we could buy an awful lot of compasses and maps," he pointed out. "Still, you're right. It is pretty amazing."

"Admiring all the cool stuff?" Dave said, from behind Frank's shoulder.

"Oh, hi," Joe said. "I'm really amazed at it all."

"I know," Dave replied. "Some of the boats I've seen are crammed with enough electronics to stock a store. GPS, VHF radio, radar, depth finders, loran . . . you name it. I know one guy who has to have the latest of everything. He's thrown out more gear than most people could afford to buy, just because it was last year's model. I doubt if he'd know how to work half the gadgets."

"That reminds me of something I wanted to ask you about," Joe said. "How do people afford to race these boats? Just having one of them trucked from one race to another must cost a fortune."

Dave nodded. "Believe me, it does. That's why a lot of offshore racers are people with money. Some are like Dennis Shire. It's his company that sponsors his boat. And Barry Batten is bankrolled by a group of corporate sponsors. They get to have big decals with the name of their product on the side of his boat. When he wins, millions of people see them on TV and in newspapers."

"Just like racing cars," Frank observed. "You know, I used to think that they put those names of sparkplugs and motor oils on the cars because those were the brands used in the cars. Then I saw one with the name of a soft drink on it, in big letters. That blew my theory. No way did that car run on cola!"

Dave grinned. "Of course, there are cash prizes for winning boats," he continued. "Those really help cover your costs . . . but only *if* you win. The same goes for betting. You've got to win for it to do you any good."

"Betting? On boat races?" Joe said, surprised.

"Sure. Sports betting is a big business, where it's legal. Nevada, for instance. And offshore racing is as much a sport as any other," Dave replied. "Of course, even a big national meet like this one doesn't attract the kind of bets you'd get on the Super Bowl or the America's Cup. Still, I'm sure that a lot of bucks will change hands on Saturday, depending on who wins."

Frank said, "I heard a rumor that somebody was threatening to sabotage the meet. Do you think there's anything to it?"

Dave shifted uncomfortably. After a long hesitation, he said, "Yeah, I heard that, too. But you know what I think? I figure people are spreading those rumors because they hope to spook their rivals—you know, psych them out so they won't do their best."

Hearing this, Frank felt something that was a cross between irritation and disappointment. If the supposed sabotage was nothing more than a campaign of psychological warfare, he and Joe were wasting their time. Trying to unnerve your opponents might not be very sportsmanlike, but it wasn't illegal.

"Things have been mysteriously going wrong with some of the boats, though, haven't they?" Joe asked.

"Going wrong, sure," Dave replied. "But mysteriously? I doubt it. Look, an offshore racing boat takes a terrible beating out on the water. You hit a wave at a hundred miles an hour, you might as well be hitting a wall. And our boats aren't that sturdy, either. A question of saving weight. So what happens? Things break. Last spring I was in a race with six other boats, and not one of us finished in good shape. Three didn't finish at all. Sabotage? No way—just the breaks, that's all."

"Hey, Frank, we'd better go," Joe said. "It's nearly two. Dennis Shire is taking us for a ride," he added to Dave.

"Way cool," Dave said. "*Adelita* is really fast. Maybe not quite fast enough to beat Barry, but fast. I'll walk you out to the dock."

They edged through the crowd to the marina entrance and showed their passes to the guard. As they walked out toward Dennis's slip, Dave pointed out some of the boats that would be contending for prizes in their various classes.

"Look," Joe said in a low voice. "Isn't that Batten up ahead?"

Frank looked. The top contender had changed into a high-visibility orange jumpsuit. The guy walking next to him was wearing a matching jumpsuit and carrying two bright orange crash helmets.

"They must be going out for a practice run," Dave remarked. "That's his throttleman, Chuck Aurora, with him."

At that moment, Joe let out a startled exclamation.

Up ahead, Batten's throttleman was bent almost double, clutching his middle. He let go of the two helmets, which echoed hollowly as they fell onto the dock. One of them rolled slowly across the wooden planks and over the edge. Just as Frank heard the splash, the stricken throttleman let out a groan and collapsed.

Batten looked around and spotted Dave and the Hardys. "Hey!" he shouted. "Come help me! I think Chuck's been poisoned!"

5 Suspicious Shrimp

Joe sprinted along the dock and knelt down next to the groaning throttleman. Putting his arm around the man's shoulders, he demanded, "Are you all right? Do you need a doctor?"

"Stomach," the man gasped, looking at him with pleading eyes. "Cramps. It's killing me."

Joe glanced around. Frank and Dave were rushing up to help. Barry Batten watched for a moment, then moved over to the edge of the dock. What was he up to? Joe kept an eye on him, as Batten picked up a boat hook and bent down to fish for something in the harbor.

"Got it!" Barry said. He straightened up. The orange helmet that had fallen in the water was suspended from the end of the boat hook.

41

"What's wrong?" Frank asked Joe, studying Chuck's pale face.

"Stomach cramps," Joe replied. "We ought to get help for him."

Dave said, "I'll go tell the guards to call the first aid squad." He turned and started for the head of the dock.

Barry came over, the dripping helmet dangling by his side. "You two again! Every time I've had a problem today, you guys were around. I'm starting to wonder if maybe you're bad luck."

Joe thought of saying that Barry obviously brought his own problems with him. Then he reminded himself that he and Frank were in the middle of an investigation. Carrying on a feud with one of the important figures in the case would not be very professional.

Instead, he asked, "What was it your friend swallowed? The paramedics will need to know."

"Why ask me?" Barry replied crossly.

"You're the one who said he was poisoned," Frank pointed out. "With what?"

Barry reddened. "*I* don't know. It just looked that way to me, that's all."

"It must have been that shrimp salad we ate at the inn," Chuck said faintly. "I told you it tasted funny. You're lucky you didn't have any."

"I think somebody *put* something in that shrimp salad," Barry said, glaring at Joe and Frank. "And

I think it was meant for me. But don't worry, I'm going to be on my guard from now on."

"Barry, that's crazy," Chuck objected.

Barry raised one eyebrow. "Is it? Remember, I carried both our plates to the table, then went back for iced tea. Anybody could have put something in your food, thinking it was mine."

"Can you think of any reason for somebody to do that?" Frank asked.

"To keep me from winning, what else?" Barry replied. "Somebody must have figured out that he can't hope to beat me by playing fair. Or maybe he's working for some bookie who took a lot of bets on me and wants to make sure I don't win so that he doesn't have to pay off."

"Aw, come on, Barry," Chuck started to say.

"Or, hey, what about that nut who threatened me? *She* came through the dining room," Barry continued. "You know, the whale lover. That's why she was so sure I'm not going to win."

"Did either of you see anyone stop by your table?" Frank asked.

Chuck shook his head.

Barry hesitated and rubbed his square jaw. "Well, no," he said, with what sounded like regret. "But they would have waited until my back was turned, wouldn't they?"

Joe heard running footsteps and looked around. Dave was returning, with two uniformed medics.

One, a man, was wheeling a stretcher. The other, a woman, was carrying a first aid chest. Joe stood up and backed away from Chuck to give them room.

The medics checked over Chuck's condition, then lifted him onto the stretcher. His forehead was beaded with sweat, but Joe thought he looked better than he had just a few minutes before.

"Take it easy, pal. Don't worry about a thing," Barry said. Then he turned abruptly to Dave. "I need a new throttleman. What do you say?"

Dave looked stunned, Joe noticed. Dave hadn't expected to be able to race at all. Now he was being offered a spot on what was probably the winning team.

"Uh . . . sure, Barry," Dave stammered as the medics wheeled Chuck away. "Sure, great!"

Barry handed him the damp helmet. "Come on, then. I want to get some practicing in."

He walked away without another glance at Joe and Frank. Dave gave them a dazed look and said, "Later, guys," then followed Barry.

After a short silence, Joe said, "What a toad that Barry is. Couldn't he have waited until they'd taken Chuck away before he asked Dave?"

"I wonder what'll happen when Chuck recovers," Frank replied. "Either he or Dave is in for a lot of grief."

Joe looked at his brother. "I hate to say this, but you don't think Dave . . . ?"

Frank knew what Joe was getting at and shook

44

his head. "Poisoned Chuck to get a shot at the race? Nah. Dave seemed genuinely shocked. Besides, he'd have no guarantee that Barry wouldn't ask someone else."

"Good," Joe said. "Because he and Dennis strike me as the only nice guys around this competition."

"And we're going to miss our ride in Dennis's boat," Frank said, breaking into a sprint. "Come on!"

They found Dennis standing on the dock next to slip B-48, stroking his beard and looking irritated. Frank explained why they were late.

"That's a shame," Dennis said. "As soon as we get back, I'll have to find out how Chuck's doing."

Joe and Frank put on the flotation jackets and helmets he gave them. They met his throttleman, a dark-haired guy of about twenty-five named Miguel, then got their first good look at the boat. *Adelita* was big, at least as long and wide as a good-size truck. The hull was mostly white, with wavy stripes of red and green along the sides. There were just four places in the cockpit, two in front and two in back, surrounded by a Plexiglas windscreen.

Joe climbed into one of the rear seats and fastened the shoulder harness. Frank settled next to him and said, "Do you think they'll give us parachutes?"

Joe grinned. Frank was right. This felt more like

45

an F-16 fighter plane than a boat. Miguel fired up the two supercharged V-8 engines, and they moved slowly out of the marina into the harbor.

Frank could see that it was Miguel's job to operate the lever controlling the speed of the engine while Dennis was at the wheel. The deep rumble from the exhausts echoed in Frank's chest and seemed to hint at incredible power waiting to be unleashed.

They passed Geller's Neck and crossed into the open waters of the bay. As the boat started to rock in the waves, Dennis turned toward Miguel and nodded once. The engine note mounted to a roar. It was as if a giant hand were pressing Joe back into his seat. The bow of the boat rose, blocking his view ahead. Looking to the side, through the rainbow-streaked curtain of spray, he saw that the entire boat was riding two or three feet higher now. They were "on the step." Instead of floating *in* the water, they were planing *on* the water. Only the tip of the stern and the two propellers were touching the surface.

Joe tapped Frank on the shoulder, grinned, and gave him a thumbs-up. No point in trying to shout over the racket of the engines. He was about to try some sign language when, without even slowing, Dennis made a sweeping turn to starboard. The boat heeled over so far that Joe was almost afraid he would fall out. Then it leveled off, just in time for the bow to smash into an oncoming wave. The shock threw Joe forward. Only the safety harness kept his head from slamming into the back of Miguel's seat. Joe caught his breath, then met Frank's eye again. This time his grin was a little weaker.

All too soon they were back in the harbor, putt-putting toward the marina. Dennis nosed *Adelita* into the slip, and Miguel threw the gear lever into reverse, blipping the throttles just enough to bring the big boat to a dead halt. Then he jumped onto the dock, taking one of the bowlines with him. In minutes the boat was securely moored and the four were standing on the dock.

"That was fantastic," Frank told Dennis. "Compared to our little runabout, it was like riding in a Formula One race car instead of a tired old family sedan."

Dennis smiled. "Don't knock your runabout. You can take your friends out for a relaxing Sunday on the water, if you want. Not me. This beast of mine was built with one single thing in mind— winning races."

"And that's what she'll do on Saturday," Miguel said.

"We'll see," Dennis replied. "With some decent wave heights, we might have a pretty good chance. Barry's the one to beat, and his boat doesn't handle rough water as well as *Adelita*."

"How fast were we going today?" Frank asked.

Dennis shrugged. "No more than eighty-five on the straightaways," he said. "I was holding it in."

Joe whistled. "Weren't you afraid of getting a ticket?" he asked.

"There's no speed limit on open water," Dennis said with a grin. "That's the main reason people buy these boats. They're one of the last ways around that you can really let 'er rip."

Dennis bent down to check one of the stern lines. As he did, his folder of charts slipped out of his hand. The navigational maps spilled out and started to blow across the dock. Joe and Frank scrambled to help Dennis grab them before they skated into the water.

Joe stopped one of the folded maps with his foot and bent over to pick it up. He froze with his fingers just inches away from it. Tucked into the chart was a paper that looked very familiar. He reached down and pulled it out.

Just as he thought. It was the Earthquest leaflet, with a skull and crossbones drawn near the bottom. But this time the scrawled words read: "Polluters Die—And You're Next."

6 Dennis Menaced

Something about the stillness of Joe's posture alerted Frank. With two quick strides he was next to Joe. In a low voice, he asked, "What's the matter?"

Wordlessly, Joe held up the leaflet.

"What's that?" Dennis asked, coming over to join them. After looking at the leaflet, he added, "Where'd you get that?"

"It was tucked into one of your maps," Joe told him. "This one."

Dennis took the map and glanced at it. "Manasquam Inlet," he said, scratching his beard. "I haven't used that chart in weeks. That leaflet could have been sitting there a long time."

"I'm afraid not," Frank responded. "I happen

to know that Earthquest just printed up those flyers recently . . . without the threatening message at the bottom, though. Where do you usually keep your maps? In the boat?"

Dennis shook his head. "I don't leave anything in *Adelita*. There's no safe place for stuff, so I lock everything in the trunk of my car."

"You mean that folder of maps was locked up until just before we went out in the boat?" Joe asked.

"No, I had it with me earlier. I wanted to use my lunch hour to get more familiar with the waters off Bayport," Dennis replied.

"So you took the folder to lunch at the inn," Frank said. "Did you leave it at your table while you went to the buffet?"

Dennis frowned in concentration. "You know, I think I must have," he finally said. "I don't really recall. I did talk to Magnusson on my way back to the table, though, and I can't see myself juggling my plate, glass, and silverware with a portfolio tucked under my arm."

Joe asked, "Can you think of any other time today when the folder was out of your sight?"

Dennis's frown deepened, and his eyes shifted back and forth from Frank to Joe. "Say, you guys do a good imitation of detectives, don't you?" he said. It seemed to Frank that there was a new coolness in his voice.

"Anyway, the answer's no," Dennis continued. "Whoever put that thing in my map folder must have done it during lunchtime. Any more questions? Because Miguel and I have work to do."

Frank glanced at Joe, then said, "No, that's all I can think of, Dennis. Thanks for the ride. We'll see you later."

He and Joe handed Dennis the maps they'd rescued, then left. As they started down the dock, Joe said, "There's another possibility, you know."

"You mean that Dennis may have put the leaflet there himself and wrote those words on it?" Frank said. "I know, I thought of that. But if he did, what was he planning to do with it? Slip it to someone else? Or pretend to find it, so we'd all think that he's a target of the harassment, too?"

Joe let out a sigh. "I wish that, just once, we'd find ourselves investigating a case that was simple and straightforward."

Frank grinned. "You mean, like, 'Mister, Stevie took my bike and won't give it back. Will you get it for me?' Let's face it, if we did get a case like that, it'd turn out that the bike was really Stevie's after all and that a criminal gang wanted it because some rival crooks had hidden the floor plans for the local bank inside the handlebars!"

"I guess you're right," Joe said with a laugh. "Hey, look, there's Susan Shire. Why don't we try to get some information from her?"

51

Dennis's ex-wife didn't look much like a glamorous TV star at that moment. She was bending over the open engine hatch of a sleek metallic purple boat. Her hair was pulled back roughly into a ponytail, she was wearing a big T-shirt stained with grease, and she had a big black smudge on one cheek. Frank called to her.

"Who—" Susan said, straightening up. She was holding a flashlight in one hand and a small screwdriver in the other. She recognized Joe. "Oh, it's you. The one who rescued Dennis this morning, when I shoved him in the water. I should thank you . . . I guess."

"Don't mention it," Joe said wryly. He pointed with his chin toward the boat engines. "Are you having problems?"

Susan gave a short laugh. "Does a duck quack?" she demanded in return. "Look at it this way, these engines are incredible *if* every one of a few hundred delicate parts works exactly the way they're supposed to. And if some of them *don't* do what they're supposed to, all you've got is a very big, very expensive boat anchor."

"This morning Dennis seemed to think somebody had been messing with his engines," Frank said.

"Well, aren't you the little diplomat," Susan replied, with a lopsided grin. "He accused *me* of doing it, in case you missed that part of the scene. Believe me—Dennis never was very good at recognizing his own shortcomings. And as for accepting responsibility for them, well, what can I say!"

"I've heard other people complain about somebody messing with their boats, though," Frank said, stretching the truth a little. "There's talk that somebody's out to sabotage the meet."

"I guess it's possible," Susan said. "There are all kinds of crazies out there. But if you ask me, people who say things like that are just making excuses for themselves in advance."

"Did you hear about Chuck, Barry Batten's throttleman?" Joe said. "He got bad stomach cramps and had to be taken off by the first-aid squad. He thought it was the shrimp salad at lunch, but Barry claimed he'd been poisoned."

Susan rolled her eyes theatrically. "That Barry!" she exclaimed. "I stopped listening to that stuff about five minutes after I met him. He is a classic paranoid. And he's also unbelievably superstitious . . . Anything that happens, he's convinced it's connected to him. Too bad about Chuck, but he shouldn't have risked that shrimp salad. It looked to me as if it had been sitting out too long."

Joe was about to ask another question when Susan added, "Sorry, fellows, but I don't have any more time to chitchat. I've got a lot of work to do." She turned back to the engines.

Frank and Joe walked away. "So," Joe said in an undertone, "Susan Shire had lunch at the inn also.

53

She could have put that leaflet in Dennis's mapcase to bug him. They obviously don't get along."

"Maybe," Frank said. "But whoever was responsible for Dennis's leaflet had to know about the other one, the one that Magnusson got this morning. And the two are so much alike that they probably came from the same person. I can see why Susan might decide to do something to shake up Dennis. But would she go to all the trouble of faxing that other leaflet to the meet office first?"

Joe scratched his head. "Well, she might . . . if it was part of a bigger plan to ruin the meet," he suggested.

"Okay, sure," Frank replied, frowning. "But what motive would she have for doing that? I get the impression that she's expected to do well in the big race. Why wreck it?"

"*I* don't know," Joe said, frustration showing in his voice. "It's just a theory. What we need now are a lot more facts."

Frank nodded decisively. "Right. And the best way to get them is to talk to the people who have them. Let's head over to the inn and do a little high-level mingling."

Joe and Frank made sure to get home in time to set the table for dinner. Afterward, Laura Hardy, their mother, said, "I'm off to a meeting of the neighborhood improvement committee. We're going to try to get a traffic light put in at that corner by the elementary school."

"Good luck," Aunt Gertrude said. "As for me, I'm going to watch a rerun of one of my favorite shows. Boys, would you care to join me?"

"Sorry, Aunt Gertrude," Joe said with a smile. "I'm allergic to black-and-white television. It makes me break out in colored spots."

Frank said, "We'll clear up. Then we have to put in some work on our latest case."

It didn't take the two brothers long to wash and dry the dishes and clean the kitchen counters. Soon they were back at the dinner table with a supply of felt-tip pens and index cards.

Frank started by making a card for each of the important people in the case. "Okay," he said when he had finished. "What do we know so far?"

Joe took the deck of cards, thumbed through it, and stopped at Barry Batten. "A lot of people think Batten is a royal pain in the neck," he said. "They also think that he's going to win the cup on Saturday."

"Unless a black cat crosses his path or something," Frank pointed out. "The one thing they all mentioned was how superstitious he is. Remember that story about the time he dropped out of a race because he didn't like his horoscope in the newspaper?"

"He's pretty cold-blooded, too," Joe said. "Did you notice that with his friend Chuck lying there

55

sick, all he cared about was fishing his helmet out of the water, and then finding a replacement for Chuck? It wouldn't surprise me if *he* poisoned Chuck's shrimp salad."

Frank said, "Let's not go overboard, Joe. In that case, why would he make a big deal of telling us Chuck had been deliberately poisoned? Why not let us assume that it was food poisoning?"

"Oh. Yeah. Well, anyway . . ." Joe flipped to the next card. "Dennis. He seems like a really nice guy. But two different people mentioned how furious he is that Susan wins more races than he does."

Frank clasped his hands behind his head and leaned back to gaze at the ceiling. "How about this?" he said. "Dennis wants to make sure Susan loses. But if he simply does something to her boat, it'll be really obvious that he's the one who's responsible. So he creates a whole campaign of sabotage as a smoke screen."

"That's clever," Joe said. "A long shot, but we should keep it in mind. For Dennis as well as his ex-wife. How about Carl Newcastle? He's one of the few racers who's actually from Bayport. He owns a big trucking company here in town. The company picks up the bills for his racing. Nobody seems to know what he and Barry were squabbling about this morning."

Frank made a note to look into this further.

Then he said, "Who's next? Connie? She obviously had the opportunity to fax that leaflet to Magnusson. She said she had them printed yesterday. And she was in the dining room at lunchtime today, according to Batten, so she could have doctored Chuck's food and slipped that second leaflet into Dennis's mapcase. Also, she doesn't even bother to hide her motive. I'd like to find out what she meant by saying that she'd make sure the big race wouldn't take place."

"Just sounding off, if you ask me," Joe replied. "What about Angelo? Same motive as Connie, and he seems like a real hothead."

"We can't place him in the dining room, though," Frank pointed out. "We'd better keep an eye on both of them. If they *are* involved, the chances are that they're working together."

"Right." Joe flipped through the cards. "That's it for now. How about a computer game? I'll spot you two power pills and an invisibility spell."

"You're on," Frank said, with a grim smile. "In other words, you're as good as dead!"

The next morning Frank decided to stay home and compile some background information on Barry, Dennis, and the others. Joe drove to the marina alone, and the first people he saw as he parked were Dennis and Miguel. Dennis waved to him and crossed the street.

"Are you ready for another little cruise?" he asked, leaning in the window of the van. "Miguel and I are on our way down to the dock right now."

"You'd better believe I am," Joe said, with a big grin. "Let's go!"

Five minutes later *Adelita* was leaving the harbor for open water. Dennis turned right and went parallel to the shoreline. As Miguel picked up the speed, he began a series of wide, easy S-turns. Joe, in the seat just behind Dennis, sat back and enjoyed the ride.

Suddenly he straightened up and frowned. He and Frank knew these waters like their own backyard. The church steeple just ahead of the starboard beam told him that they were getting close to Cooley's Ledge, a rock formation that was only inches below the surface at low tide. Why didn't Dennis turn to port to avoid the hazard? Didn't he see the warning buoy?

Then, as Dennis made a shallow turn toward the shore, Joe got a clear view of the water ahead of them. The warning buoy wasn't there. Dennis was steering right toward Cooley's Ledge, at over fifty miles an hour. He obviously didn't realize that in less than a minute the jagged rocks were going to rip the bottom out of his boat!

7 On the Rocks

"Dennis!" Joe shouted, trying to warn him about the onrushing danger. But the roar of the engines and the hiss of the water surging under the hull covered the sound of Joe's voice. He lunged forward, reaching out to grab Dennis's shoulder, but the safety harness held him trapped in his seat.

Frantic, Joe slapped the quick-release buckle of the harness. There was no time left to alert Dennis. They'd be wrecked on Cooley's Ledge before he could hope to explain. Instead, he flung himself forward, through the gap between Dennis's and Miguel's bucket seats. Grabbing the wheel with both hands, he jerked it to the left, throwing the boat into a hard turn to port.

As the boat heeled over sharply, Dennis fought

Joe for control of the wheel. He thrust his elbow toward Joe's face, but Joe's helmet protected him. Joe kept the wheel cranked over to port until he was sure that the bow was pointing away from the danger. Then he let go and fell back into his seat, just as Miguel throttled back the engines.

In the sudden silence, Joe heard Dennis yell, "Joe, are you out of your mind? You could have killed us!"

"I saved our lives," Joe replied, after taking a deep breath. He felt exhausted by the strain and his effort. "Look at your chart. We were headed straight for a dangerous ledge. There's supposed to be a warning buoy, but it isn't there. I don't know why."

Dennis narrowed his eyes at Joe. Then he took out the chart and looked back and forth between the markings there and the surroundings.

"You're right," he said at last. "Thanks, Joe. This area is terribly dangerous. Without a marker there, someone who doesn't know these waters as well as you do could easily go aground. We'd better get back and let the authorities know about this, before somebody gets badly hurt."

Back at the marina, Dennis went to the harbormaster's office to report the missing buoy. Joe found a pay phone and called Frank.

"I'd better come get you," Joe said, after explaining what had happened. "I know buoys do slip their cables now and then. But we haven't had any storms or heavy seas in the last week or two to account for it. If you ask me, somebody did it deliberately."

"It sounds that way," Frank replied. "We'd better track down the person responsible, and fast, before he or she causes a serious accident. I'll be waiting out front."

As they drove back toward the harbor, Frank said, "The first thing we need to do is find out when the buoy drifted away. Until we know that, we won't have a hope of figuring out who helped it along."

"What are the chances that we'll find anybody who saw it go?" Joe asked skeptically. "That'd be too good to be true."

"I know that," Frank replied. "But we know it was gone this morning. If we can pin down the last time somebody saw it there . . . The trouble is, most of the people who are here for the meet probably don't know this part of the sound well enough to notice whether one particular buoy is there or not."

Joe thought hard. "The charter boats!" he suddenly exclaimed, snapping his fingers. "They take fishing parties out every morning and lots of evenings, too. And the guys who work them know these waters better than we know our own backyard."

"Great idea, Joe," Frank said. He glanced at his

wrist. "And they should be coming in from their morning trips just about now, too."

Joe drove past the marina and parked near the head of Commercial Pier. He and Frank walked out on the pier, stopping at each fishing boat to ask the crew if they had passed Cooley's Ledge lately. They struck out with the first three boats. All had headed east, in the opposite direction from the ledge, after leaving the harbor.

The fourth boat they came to was Captain Bill Mares's *Susie II.* Captain Bill, in wrinkled khakis and a baseball cap, listened to their question. Then he said, "Now, there's an odd thing. That buoy was definitely there yesterday around sunset. I happened to pay attention because there was one of those big inflatable outboard rigs tied up to it. You don't see that many of them around here. And now that you ask, it comes back to me that it *wasn't* there at daybreak. I noticed without really noticing, if you catch my drift."

"So the buoy must have come loose at some time during the night," Frank said, partly to himself.

"Well, now, that's an odd thing, too," Captain Bill remarked. "It was pretty solidly anchored. I know, because I helped put it in place. It was attached to a big concrete block by a steel cable."

"How strong a cable?" Joe asked.

Captain Bill took off his cap, scratched his head, and put the cap back on. "I wouldn't hazard a guess as to its breaking strength," he said. "But it was the sort of cable you might use to lock up your bicycle, if you liked your bicycle a lot."

Joe looked over at Frank. They both knew how easily a bolt-cutting tool could slice through even the strongest bike cable lock.

"Isn't it unusual for a boat to be tied up to the buoy?" Frank asked.

"Not really," Captain Bill replied. "There's pretty fair fishing around Cooley's Ledge, and it's easier to tie up your boat to the buoy than to drop an anchor. The boat itself was a little unusual, though. Must have been about a twenty-footer, with a hefty outboard on the back. Now that I think of it, I've seen it before, it or its twin. Over to the marina. One of those ecological groups takes people out in it to teach them about eco-systems or something."

"Connie!" Joe said under his breath.

"Thanks, Captain," Frank said. "You've been a big help."

The Hardys hurried to the van and drove back to the marina. They checked the sidewalk in front of the inn, but there was no sign of Connie or Angelo. The guard at the marina gate looked in his directory and told them where the Earthquest boat was docked, but when they reached the slip, it was empty.

Joe looked around. There was a white cabin

63

cruiser moored in the next slip. A man and woman were having coffee at the small table in the cockpit.

"Ahoy," Joe called, feeling a little silly as he said it. "Did you see the Earthquest boat this morning?"

"Sure," the man said. "Connie and a friend of hers took it out about an hour ago. They wanted to check out the course for the races and find a good spot to watch from."

"Thanks," Joe called. He turned to Frank and said in a low voice, "Connie wants to stop the races. Why would she want to go looking for a spot to watch them?"

"I think we'd better ask *her* that question," Frank replied. "The sooner the better. Good thing *Sleuth* has a full tank of gas."

The two Hardys walked quickly to the farthest dock, where they kept their little runabout. It took only moments to get the engine started. Frank took the helm. Joe untied the dock lines, then jumped in.

"Where to?" he asked, as *Sleuth*'s bow turned toward the mouth of the harbor. "There's an awful lot of water out there."

"According to her neighbor, Connie was planning to look over the course of the races," Frank reminded him. "Why don't we simply start at the starting line and follow the marker buoys?"

"The course is about twenty-five miles," Joe said. "It's going to take a while."

Frank grinned. "It's laid out in a long oval, you doofus. We can keep an eye on the return leg while we're on our way out."

The morning was mostly sunny but not too warm, perfect conditions to be out on the water. The sparkling blue surface of the bay was dappled here and there by purple cloud shadows. Joe sat back in his seat and took in a lungful of the salt-tinged breeze. He half wished that he and Frank were simply taking a ride for the fun of it. Then he reminded himself that part of what he felt was the excitement of the chase. Connie and Angelo were up to something, he was sure of that. But they hadn't counted on having Frank and Joe Hardy on their trail.

Frank broke in on his brother's thoughts, saying, "Those buoys must mark the start and finish line." He steered between the two bright yellow markers. "Ready, set, *go!*" he added, shoving the throttle all the way.

The nimble runabout took off between twin sheets of spray. As the bow lifted, Joe sat up straighter to get a better view of where they were going. The next yellow buoy was already in sight. So was a sport fishing boat that was approaching them bow-on. Frank backed off the throttle and turned a few degrees to starboard. The fishing boat moved to its starboard, too, following the rules of the road that allowed the two boats to pass each other safely. As soon as he was past the other boat, Frank picked up speed again.

"See anything?" he called, over the noise of the engine.

Joe shook his head. He had grabbed a pair of binoculars from the locker, but he was having trouble holding them steady with the boat under way. He scanned the area ahead of them. Good thing it was a weekday, he thought, since it meant there weren't that many pleasure boats out. Most of them he could eliminate on the basis of their profiles. Then he noticed a low, dark shape about a mile away, almost dead ahead. He studied it as the motion of the waves made it vanish and reappear. It didn't seem to be moving.

Joe tapped Frank on the shoulder and pointed. Frank nodded, then adjusted his course to pass close to the other boat. As they drew nearer and the outlines of the boat became easier to make out, Joe became more and more sure that it was their quarry. As Captain Bill had said, there weren't often that many big inflatables in the area.

"That's Connie and Angelo," Joe announced when they were about a hundred yards away. "But what are they up to?"

He could see that Connie was kneeling in the bottom of the boat, leaning way out over the side. Angelo was crouched next to her, with something long and narrow in his hands. As *Sleuth* drew nearer, he straightened up and glanced over his shoulder, then sprang to the controls. The engine must have been idling in neutral. Almost instantly, it roared to life. The boat surged forward.

Then, just as Frank shoved *Sleuth*'s throttle all the way open, the motor on the rubber boat stalled. A passing wave slowly turned it broadside, directly in the path of the Hardys' speedboat.

Joe saw Angelo leap toward the stern of the boat and tug at the motor's manual starter, frantically trying to get his boat out of the way of the larger boat barreling toward it. Connie was thrown off balance by the sudden shift in the boat, and with a cry for help, she tumbled into the water.

"Look out, Frank!" Joe shouted, seeing Connie fall in headfirst. "Turn! We're going to hit them!"

8 Collision Course

All Frank's attention had been focused on overtaking the other boat. Now, suddenly, he had to avoid running into it—and Connie! Clenching his jaw, Frank used his left hand to turn the wheel hard to starboard, while his right hand fell to the throttle and eased it back to idle speed. *Sleuth* bucked like a startled stallion and heeled to the right. It missed the smaller boat by only a few feet.

Just then a wave rolled under the bow, catching it at an angle. For one moment Frank was sure that the boat was about to become airborne. Then the bow slapped itself down on the water. Frank felt the force of the impact in his spine and the base of his skull.

He twisted his head to look over his shoulder. "Joe?" he called. "Are you okay?"

Joe was on his knees, clutching the chrome railing. He managed a grin and called back, "Sure. I love water rides!"

Sleuth came to a halt and began to rock from side to side in the swell. From behind him, Frank heard the sudden racket of a big outboard motor. When he turned to look, Connie had scrambled back into the boat, and she and Angelo were speeding away. There was already fifty yards of open water between *Sleuth* and the big black inflatable, and the gap was widening fast.

"Are we going after them?" Joe asked.

Frank thought for a moment. "I don't think so," he said. "We know where to find them, after all. And I'm very curious to find out what they were up to out here. They weren't scouting for a spot to watch the races from, that's for sure!"

"They were obviously monkeying with the marker buoy," Joe told him. "Let's have a look."

Frank steered the boat in a wide circle that brought them to just windward of the yellow buoy, then hurried to the railing as the boat drifted down to it. Leaning over the side, he grabbed the buoy and lifted it out of the water. A length of narrow cable came with it.

"Joe, look at this!" Frank said excitedly, after scanning the cable.

69

"There's a nick in it, just below the buoy," Joe said after a moment. "It looks as if somebody tried to cut the cable."

"Or was interrupted in the middle of cutting it," Frank said. "Care to guess who?"

Joe shook his head. "That's a no-brainer. I prefer challenges. We'd better go back and tell the race officials about this."

Frank kept the engine at full revs on the way back. The noise kept him from talking to Joe, but it didn't keep him from thinking. They couldn't accuse Connie and Angelo of the sabotage. They hadn't actually seen the two cutting the cable. But still, he and Joe could alert Magnusson, then let Connie know that she and her friends were being closely watched. If that brought their sabotage to a halt, fine. And if it didn't, he and Joe would find a way to get the evidence they needed.

As they neared Bayport, they passed more and more boats. A couple of miles from harbor, Frank saw a cabin cruiser headed the other way that had a big Official sign taped to its side. He slowed down and gave Joe a questioning look.

"That must be one of the check boats getting on station for this afternoon's time trials," Joe said, after a look at his watch.

"I forgot all about them," Frank confessed. "I hope we don't have any trouble finding Magnusson. We've got to warn him about Connie."

They docked *Sleuth* in its usual spot, double-checked the lines, and walked quickly toward the exit from the marina. They were almost to the gate when Frank saw Dave Hayman and Barry Batten coming in their direction. Their bright orange jumpsuits were splotched all over with oil stains.

"What happened to you guys?" Joe asked Dave.

"A burst engine seal," Dave told him. "We'd just fired up the engines when it happened. If it had happened while we were under way, we might have burnt out the engine. As it is, it's just messy. We were pretty lucky, I guess."

Frank glanced over at Joe and raised one eyebrow. Another "accident"?

"Lucky?" Barry said, frowning. "There's nothing lucky about this meet. It's jinxed. I've got half a mind to pull out of it."

A look of alarm crossed Dave's face. Frank wasn't surprised. If Barry carried out his threat to withdraw from the race, there went Dave's big break.

"Hey, come on, Barry, accidents happen," Dave said soothingly. "Let's go get cleaned up and get ready for the time trials. You watch—we're going to blow the doors off the competition."

"Huh," Barry grunted, and walked away.

Frank asked, "Have you seen Gerald Magnusson?"

"Yeah, about fifteen minutes ago," Dave replied. "He and a bunch of VIPs were on their way to board the judges' boat. It's that big motor yacht

71

that's tied up at the end of the dock. They're having a buffet lunch on board before the time trials start."

"We'd better try to catch him," Frank told Joe.

"Right," Joe replied. "But, Dave? Just one thing—whatever happened with that guy Chuck, the one who got sick? Is he okay?"

Dave looked down at the ground. "Oh, he's a lot better today," he said. "But he won't be in any shape to race for a while. If we turn in a good time this afternoon, Barry's promised to let me be his throttleman for the next few meets. I'd better go. He doesn't like to be kept waiting."

Frank looked around. Barry was standing near the gate with his hands on his hips. Dave ran to join him. The two crossed the street, with Dave making obvious gestures of apology.

"I don't envy Dave," Joe said, as he and Frank turned and walked out the dock. "I know he's getting something he wants a lot, but it looks to me like he's paying a big price for it."

"I know," Frank said. "I wonder what he's so nervous about. Just the strain of keeping Barry happy? Or is it something more—"

A gruff voice broke in. "Hold it right there. Where do you kids think you're going?"

Frank looked up in surprise. The man who was blocking their way was built like a piano mover, with a barrel chest and a belly that overhung his belt. Over one pocket of his dark green shirt was a sewn-on patch that read Newcastle Trucking. Over the other was embroidered the name Skip.

"What's it to you?" Joe replied, irritated. "We've got official passes. See?" Joe held up the pass Magnusson had given him.

"Everybody and his uncle has official passes around here," Skip said, not even sparing a glance at the piece of pasteboard. "Pass or no pass, you keep your distance from that boat, get it?"

He pointed to the slip on his left. The boat was dark green, the same shade as the man's uniform. Its twin canopies looked as if they'd been lifted from a pair of F-16s. The only decorations were the boat's number, D-19, and the words *Newcastle Trucking*.

"Nice-looking boat," Frank said. "Pretty fast, too, huh?"

"Never mind whether it's fast or not," the man growled. "The boss doesn't want anybody hanging around here, okay? Now move it, before I decide to move it for you."

"I guess your boss just bought the marina, right?" Joe replied. "Funny, there wasn't anything in the paper about it."

Skip bristled. "Listen, wise guy—" he began.

Frank tugged at Joe's arm and said, "Come on, Joe. We've got more urgent things to do than hang around talking to this . . . friendly gentleman."

As the two Hardys walked away, Frank looked over his shoulder and called cheerfully, "Have a

73

nice day!" He wished he could have gotten a snapshot of the guy's expression. It would have made a great Halloween card.

They hadn't gone more than a few yards farther when Joe said, "Um—Frank? Guess what. No yacht."

Joe was right. The docking space at the end was vacant. "They must be having their VIP lunch out on the water," Frank guessed. "Lucky them. I guess warning Magnusson will have to wait. Let's hope that the swim Connie took will scare her into giving up her plans, whatever they are."

They turned around just in time to see Dennis walking toward them. There was a bounce in his step, and a smile peeked through his beard.

"Hey, guys," he said. "Aren't you planning to watch the time trials?"

"Sure, but I'm still not too clear what they're for," Joe confessed.

Dennis's smile widened. "I'm not surprised. This meet *is* pretty complicated, what with the different classes and different flights in each race. But let's say we forget about the small fry and just pay attention to the big boats. There are too many for them all to race safely at the same time. So the race committee decided to narrow down the field, from eleven boats to just six."

"How?" Frank asked.

"A couple of ways," Dennis replied. "The fastest boat in today's trials is automatically in, at pole position. Then there are two elimination heats. The first two boats in each of them get a spot in Saturday's race."

"That's just five entries," Joe pointed out.

"Good counting," Dennis said with a grin. "The boats that came in third and fourth in each elimination heat get to run in the consolation heat. And the top boat in *that* one is in the big race, too."

After a moment, he added, "Not that that's much consolation. Racing is tough on a boat. After today's run, then the elimination races, the consolation winner is likely to be pretty battered."

"In other words," Frank said, "the fastest boat in the time trials doesn't race in the eliminations, and that gives it an automatic advantage in the big race on Saturday."

"You got it," Dennis replied. "Wouldn't you know I had the rotten luck to draw the number one spot for the time trials."

"Is that a bad thing?" Joe asked.

Dennis made a face. "Believe it. What you want to do is go just fast enough to beat the others, but without straining your engines. But if you don't know how fast the others go, because they haven't gone yet . . . well, you get the idea.

"I'd better get moving," he continued. "Hey, why don't you bring your boat around and follow me out? That way you'll get a good spot to watch."

"Great!" Frank said. "We'll be right back."

He and Joe hurried to *Sleuth* and got under way. They reached the other side of the marina just as the sharklike shape of *Adelita* nosed out of its slip, moving barely faster than a walk. Frank circled around and came onto a course parallel to the other boat. Dennis waved one hand in a circle, then pointed toward open water. A V of white water began to form under the bow as *Adelita* picked up speed. Frank adjusted his throttle to keep pace with Dennis. He sat back and smiled as the breeze ruffled his hair.

They were coming abreast of the harbor mouth when Joe let out a startled shout. Frank looked around. What was wrong?

Just at that moment, a gigantic ball of orange flame surged up from the stern of Dennis's boat.

9 Racing the Clock

The flames billowed up from *Adelita*'s engine compartment, topped by a growing column of black smoke. For one moment Joe was too startled to react. Then he lunged forward and grabbed *Sleuth*'s fire extinguisher from its bracket on the forward bulkhead.

"Pull alongside!" he shouted to Frank. As the distance between the two boats narrowed, Joe shifted the extinguisher to his left hand and picked up a boat hook. The instant he was close enough for the long pole to reach, he hooked the other boat's gunwale, pulled the two craft closer together, and leaped across the foaming gap onto the deck of the racing boat.

Miguel had already managed to unlatch the

cover of the engine compartment. He used a long-handled wrench to raise it a few inches, while Dennis sprayed foam through the opening. Joe pointed the horn of his extinguisher at the opening, too, and pressed the thumb lever. The hiss of the two extinguishers was even louder than the angry rumble of the fire. The color of the smoke shifted to white, and suddenly the flames vanished.

Joe and Dennis continued to spray the engines with foam for another thirty seconds or so. Then, as if on signal, they both stopped at the same moment. The only sound was the slap of the waves on the side of the boat and the muffled putt-putt from *Sleuth*'s idling motor.

"Whew!" Dennis said, wiping his forehead. "That was nasty. Thanks for your help, Joe."

"I think we skip the time trials," Miguel observed.

"I think you're right," Dennis said in a choked voice.

Joe asked, "Does that mean you're out of the race?"

Dennis shrugged and continued to stare down at the engines. "It depends on how much damage was done. If we can get the engines back in shape fast enough, we can still run in one of the elimination heats tomorrow and get a spot that way."

"What happened?" Joe continued.

"I'd like to know the answer to that one myself," Dennis replied. "You think you guys could give us a tow back to the dock?"

Joe swallowed. He was ready to try, and he knew Frank would be, too. But taking a forty-foot boat under tow in a crowded harbor was no job for casual boaters. Luckily, before he had to answer Dennis's request, a tugboat approached. Its captain had seen the smoke and offered to help. Miguel scrambled up to *Adelita*'s bow, caught the towline, and fastened it securely to the bow cleat. Then he raised his clasped hands over his head to signal to the tugboat crew that the tow was securely attached.

The note of the other boat's powerful diesels rose in pitch. The thick rope came dripping out of the water and straightened out. For a long moment, nothing seemed to happen. Joe realized that the line must be stretching. Would it hold? Then *Adelita* started to move.

Joe looked around. Frank was following at a safe distance. He caught Joe's glance and waved. Now that the emergency was past, Joe began to wonder. Had the fire been an accident? Or was it part of a real and increasingly dangerous plan to wreck the regatta?

Once back at the dock, Joe helped Dennis and Miguel maneuver *Adelita* into its slip. Frank tied up *Sleuth* nearby and joined them, just as a blond guy in white coveralls came running up.

79

"Dennis!" he exclaimed. "I heard what happened. Are you two okay?"

"We're fine," Dennis replied. "I'm not so sure about the engines, though. Joe, Frank—meet Pavel, one terrific mechanic."

The Hardys said hi to Pavel, who nodded briefly and went immediately to the boat's engine compartment. Pulling a small, powerful flashlight from a side pocket, he shone the beam on the soot-blackened engines.

"It's not too bad, thanks to the automatic fire-extinguishing system," Pavel said after a few moments. "The fuel cutoff worked, too, I see. That's good. One of the fuel lines became loose. If the flow had not stopped at once, we'd still be watching the flames."

"A loose fuel line?" Dennis questioned, his voice heavy with disbelief. "Didn't you check those fittings when you tuned the engines this morning?"

Pavel looked up over his shoulder at Dennis. "Yes, I did. They were tight," he told him.

"Then how . . ." Dennis fell silent. It seemed to Joe that his face turned pale.

Frank asked, "Was there someone with the boat all morning?"

"What? Oh—" Dennis thought for a moment. "Let's see, we came back from that practice run where Joe saved our bacon. We hung around for a while. Then Pavel showed up to give the engines a final tweak or two. Miguel and I watched him for a little while. Then we went up to the inn to get a bite to eat. When we came back, we ran into you and Joe. So yes, somebody was here the whole time."

Joe noticed Pavel stare down at the ground, twisting his hands together. "You have a right to be very angry at me," Pavel began. "While I was working on the engines, I needed a torque wrench I had left in the car. I went back for it, and I think I might have left the engine hatch open while I was gone." Pavel ran his hands through his blond hair. "I guess you'll want to fire me for this."

Dennis stared at him. "Fire you? Don't be silly, Pavel. You're a mechanic, not a watchdog. How could you know?"

"What time was this?" Frank asked.

Pavel shrugged. "Half an hour before Dennis and Miguel returned? More? I didn't notice."

Joe looked around. All the neighboring slips were empty. Their occupants were either out watching or taking part in the time trials. "Was anybody else around at the time, Pavel?" he asked.

"I didn't notice," Pavel repeated, almost choking on his words. "I was working on the engines! That was all I paid attention to."

"Look," Dennis said to Joe and Frank, "I know you're just trying to help, but that's enough. Pavel's got a big job ahead of him, and I don't want him upset. Why don't you guys go out and watch

81

the time trials, while we try to figure out if we can fix my engines?"

"I guess we'll do that," Frank said after glancing at Joe for his agreement. "We'll see you later. Good luck with the engines."

The Hardys returned to *Sleuth* and started out again. Even before they had cleared the harbor, they could hear the distant snarl of high-powered engines running at peak revs. On the other side of what looked like a solid wall of spectator boats, the rooster tails of spray thrown up by the straining rivals glistened in the sunlight.

"We're not going to see a thing," Joe complained. "And even if we do, we won't know who won unless we find out the lap times of all the entries."

"We'll find out who won soon enough," Frank replied. "We're here to soak up atmosphere and keep an eye out for anything that might help us break this case. Besides," he added with a grin, "practically everybody we might want to question is out here. Why just sit around on the dock, waiting for them to come back, when we can have a fun afternoon on the water? See if you can find the sunblock, would you?"

It was almost six o'clock when the trials came to an end and the flotilla of boats started back to Bayport. Frank and Joe went back to shore with the crowd. Once they'd docked *Sleuth,* they walked around to Dennis's slip. They found him on the dock next to *Adelita,* sitting in a folding chair, reading a computer magazine. He looked up alertly as they approached.

"Oh, hi," he said. His shoulders relaxed. "You guys got some sun this afternoon."

Frank winced and said, "I know. We left the sunblock in the van. What's the story with your boat?"

A grim smile appeared on Dennis's lips. "Pavel says he was able to fix the damage," he reported. "We're running in the second elimination heat tomorrow. And we're going to be taking turns sitting right here until then. *Nobody* goes near *Adelita.*"

Frank was on the point of telling Dennis that he and Joe were detectives and offering to help Dennis track down the saboteur. Then he reflected that Magnusson had asked them to keep their role secret. Unless he changed his mind, Frank and Joe had an obligation to follow his wishes.

"Any word on how the time trials came out?" Joe asked. "Who won?"

Dennis made a face. *"It's Mine* took first," he said. "That's the name of Barry's boat. Fits, doesn't it? But Carl Newcastle came close to edging him out. If I'd had a chance to try, it would have been a real race. But you know what they say. It's not over till it's over."

83

A bright yellow boat powered by three big outboards entered the channel, slowed almost to a stop, and eased into the slip next to Dennis's. Once the boat was tied up, the driver, a woman in a bright yellow jumpsuit, leaped onto the dock and called, "Hey, Dennis, did you hear? We took first in our class."

"That's great, Margot," Dennis called back. "Since you don't have to race tomorrow, you can take the day off and come cheer me on."

"It's a date," Margot replied.

Joe turned to Frank and said, "I wonder . . ."

"Me too," Frank said. "Let's find out."

They walked over to Margot, who was talking to her throttleman about their run that afternoon. She looked up. The Hardys introduced themselves and congratulated her and her partner. Then Joe asked, "Before you went out this afternoon, did you happen to notice anybody hanging around Dennis's boat?"

Margot frowned. "Not to notice, no. Pavel was over there, fine-tuning the engines," she said. She turned to her throttleman. "How about you, Bob?"

Bob was a guy in his twenties, with a long, narrow face and a lock of dark hair that fell down over his forehead. "Hmm," he said. "You know, now that you mention it, I did. I noticed her going along, looking over the boats, just rubbernecking, you know? Then when she got to *Adelita*, she stopped and walked out alongside. She looked like she wanted to climb aboard and see how it felt to be at the helm."

"Did she go aboard?" Frank asked, trying to keep the urgency out of his voice.

"I can't say," Bob replied. "Sorry. I got busy with something else and stopped watching her. Cute kid, but way too young for me."

Joe asked, "What did she look like?"

Bob said, "I don't know . . . brown hair is all I really noticed. Oh . . . and she was wearing a T-shirt with a slogan on it in big letters. Something about saving the sea."

10 Connie Stonewalls

"Brown hair and an ecology T-shirt?" Joe said, as he and Frank walked quickly toward the head of the dock. "Come on, give me a break—of course it was Connie!"

"All I'm saying is, we don't know for sure," Frank replied. "We didn't see her by Dennis's boat. We don't know what she was wearing. And if somebody wanted to undermine what she and her group are doing, what better way than to get some girl in a shirt with some kind of environmental message to go around acting suspiciously?"

"Doubtful, if you ask me," Joe grumbled. "We practically caught her and Angelo red-handed this morning, and now we have a witness who saw somebody just like her casing a boat that was sabotaged. Isn't that enough?"

Frank sighed. "Enough to question her, sure," he said. "But not to accuse her. For that, we need proof."

As they crossed the street, Frank noticed a big white van parked at the curb in front of the Waterside Inn. "Look, Joe," he said. "There's a crew from *World Sports Today* here. They must be planning to do a segment on the races."

"Yeah, and look who's hoping to get equal time," Joe replied.

Just ahead were Connie, a tanned man in a blue blazer holding a microphone, and a three-person camera crew. A little half circle of spectators watched and listened. Frank and Joe joined them.

". . . crazy enough to hold a sports car race in a public park," Connie was saying. "But this is the same thing. These boats go over a hundred miles an hour, spewing exhaust fumes and spreading oil slicks across the whole bay. They call it sport. I call it pollution."

Some of the spectators started to boo. In response, others cheered. As arguments started among them, the announcer handed the mike to the sound engineer, saying, "Let's head down to the dock and get some footage of race preparations."

As the camera crew packed its gear, Frank and

Joe edged through the crowd toward Connie. Frank noticed that her T-shirt read Save the Ocean. He also noticed that it was spotless. Could she have fiddled with Dennis's engines and kept her shirt from getting oil-stained? It didn't seem likely. But then, she might have changed shirts. She probably had a whole drawer full of identical T-shirts.

Connie was talking earnestly to a woman in tennis clothes. She glanced over and saw Frank and Joe coming. Her face hardened, and she turned away, as if she had just seen something that made her feel sick.

Frank hadn't noticed Angelo in the crowd. Suddenly he was facing the Hardys, blocking their approach to Connie. His jaw was set, and his fists, though still at his sides, were clenched.

"You guys better leave us alone," he said.

"What's your problem, Angelo?" Joe demanded.

Angelo glared at him. "You're nothing but a couple of snoops," he declared. "You're working for the polluters, trying to pin something on us."

"Something like cutting the cable on that buoy this morning?" Frank asked.

"There you go," Angelo said, with a snort. "Just what I expected. Get lost, will you? We've got nothing to say to you."

Frank looked over Angelo's shoulder and met

Connie's gaze. She looked half scared, half defiant.

"Connie?" he called. "What were you doing hanging around Dennis Shire's boat today before the time trials?"

"Don't tell him a thing," Angelo spat out.

"We were there when Dennis's boat caught fire," Joe said. "It's just good luck that nobody got killed. Is that what you call protecting the environment?"

"I've got nothing to say to you sneaks," Connie replied. "You hear? Nothing!"

She turned and walked away. When Joe started after her, Angelo put out his arm to block the way. Joe looked down at the arm, then stared Angelo in the face. Before the face-off could get rough, Frank pulled Joe back.

"It's not worth starting something," he told Joe, loudly enough for Angelo to hear, too. "If they don't want to talk to us, fine. I wonder how they'll like talking to the cops instead."

Angelo glared at them for a moment, then turned and followed Connie.

"I hope we never want anything from student government," Frank said. "Come on, let's go find Magnusson. It feels like weeks since we've given him a report."

The race chairman was in his office off the lobby, talking on the phone. When he saw the

Hardys in the doorway, he placed his palm over the receiver and said, "Come in, boys. Sit down. I'll be right with you."

"Don't worry, George," he said into the telephone. "I'll have all this sorted out by Monday. Yes, I'm a hundred percent sure. I'll be back in Cleveland Sunday afternoon. If you're so anxious, you can always come by the house that evening and pick up a check. But I really think it can wait until Monday morning. Yes . . . all right. Have a good weekend."

Magnusson replaced the receiver and sighed. "Some people expect any new idea to fail, no matter how many times they're proven wrong," he remarked. "Oh well, their loss is someone else's gain. I've been hoping to see you fellows. Have you made any progress?"

"Yes and no," Frank said, after taking a chair. "We're almost certain that someone *is* trying to sabotage the meet. And we can make a pretty good guess who it is, too. The trouble is, we don't have a bit of evidence to back up our suspicions."

"Why don't you tell me about it?" Magnusson suggested, settling back in his seat.

Frank and Joe took turns telling him about the missing buoy at Cooley's Ledge, Barry Batten's broken oil seal, Dennis's loosened fuel line, and the apparent attempt by Connie and Angelo to cut loose one of the marker buoys.

"Coming on top of those threatening leaflets,"

Frank concluded, "it's pretty obvious that some-body is out to stop the meet, or at least to throw a lot of sand in the gears."

Magnusson raised an eyebrow. "Somebody? You mean Earthquest."

"It was their leaflet that was used," Frank said. "And they've made it clear that they'd *like* to see the races canceled. But that doesn't prove that they'd do anything dangerous or illegal to make it happen."

"We need more evidence," Joe added.

"Yes, I can see that," Magnusson said, nodding slowly. He glanced at his watch. "Are you lads free this evening? I'm giving a small dinner party, and I'd like it if you could join us. You might find it, ah, helpful as well as pleasant."

Frank looked over at Joe, then said, "Thank you, sir. We appreciate the invitation."

"Splendid," Magnusson said, getting to his feet. "Do you know Au Vieux Port, on Herrick's Cove? I'm told that their seafood is very good. Eight o'clock?"

"We'll be there," Frank promised.

As he and Joe left the office, Joe murmured, "That's one of the ritziest places around. We'd better run home and change!"

When Aunt Gertrude saw Joe and Frank come downstairs in sharply creased khakis, dress shirts, and freshly shined loafers, her eyebrows climbed nearly to her hairline. And when she heard where they were going, she insisted on inspecting their fingernails. Joe had to put his foot down to keep her from making sure that they had washed behind their ears.

Herrick's Cove was just fifteen minutes from the Hardy house. They pulled into Au Vieux Port's parking lot on the stroke of eight. Dave was just walking toward the entrance. He waited for them.

"Some place, huh?" he said. "I could hardly believe it when Gerald invited me. That must be one of the perks of crewing for Barry."

The restaurant was built on a wharf, over the water. From the front, it looked like a collection of weathered fishing shacks. As they neared the entrance, Joe noticed a terrace at the far side, with umbrella-topped tables that overlooked the bay.

Inside, there were fresh flowers on every table, amid sparkling china, crystal, and silver. The tuxedo-clad maître d' led them to a long table in a windowed alcove. Joe did his best to act casual, but he found himself wishing he and Frank had gone to Mr. Pizza for dinner instead.

Gerald Magnusson's "small dinner party" turned out to be about twenty people. Dennis and Miguel were there, and so were Barry, Carl Newcastle, and a lot of the other competitors. Dennis introduced the Hardys to a thin, nervous-looking guy named Pete Carnofsky. He turned out to be the driver of *Blue Flame*, the boat that had almost crashed while being trucked down Shore Road two days earlier.

The talk was all about engines, deep-V hulls versus catamarans, and tales of other races and other racers. Joe listened with half an ear. He could tell that Frank, who was seated on the other side of the table, was doing the same.

The first course was huge platters of shellfish on beds of crushed ice. Joe recognized the crabs, crawfish, and oysters, but the other varieties were a mystery. He made a point of trying everything, including a tiny, rubbery creature that he had to tease out of its shell with what looked like a metal toothpick. Then he decided to go wash his hands.

As he was coming out of the washroom, he heard a muffled man's voice say, "That's right, in the Bayport Offshore Races on Saturday. What's the line on BB? No, I don't want to place a bet now. Yes, I'm sure—one hundred percent sure. But when I do, it'll be big."

There was a click. Joe hurried forward. On the other side of a partition was a pay telephone. The cord of the receiver was still swaying back and forth, but there was no one near it. Joe peered into the dining room. Magnusson and Newcastle were standing near the table, talking. Barry was just taking his seat. Had any of them just made that phone call?

Joe thought fast. Someone was checking the

odds on the race and was planning to bet a large amount of money. He doubted that there was an illegal gambling ring in Bayport that could handle really big sums. That meant that the call had probably been long distance.

On a hunch, Joe returned to the phone, put in a quarter, and dialed "0." When the operator answered, he said, "I'd like time and charges on the call I just made, please."

"Just a moment, sir. I'll connect you to your long distance service," the operator replied.

When the next operator came on, he repeated his request. After a pause, the operator said, "Your call to area code 702 lasted three minutes, and your calling card was billed one dollar and twelve cents."

Crossing his fingers, Joe asked, "What was that number again, operator?"

"I'm sorry, sir," the operator said. "I can't release that information. Have a nice day."

Joe didn't have a chance to tell Frank about the mysterious phone call until after dinner, when they were driving home.

"I checked the phone book," he concluded. "That's the area code for Nevada. If you ask me, somebody is planning to make a big bet on Saturday's race. I just wish I'd seen who it was."

"It may not be that important," Frank said. "We already know that people bet on themselves in these races."

"Yeah, but what if somebody bets on the *other* guy, then takes a dive?" Joe pointed out.

"I see what you're saying," Frank responded. "Hmm . . . you remember Dad's friend Claude? The one who's a private investigator in Las Vegas? Why don't we give him a call when we get home and ask if he'll nose around a little?"

"Good idea," Joe said. "And why not do a database search on all the main competitors, too? We might turn up some incident in their past that'll help us figure out what's going on here."

An hour later Frank pushed his chair back from the computer table and said, "Okay, what do we have?"

Joe looked up from using a highlighter on several pages of printout. "A lot of gossip," he said. "Dennis's computer company is said to be a takeover target. Magnusson's real estate empire is supposedly having serious cash-flow problems. Newcastle's trucking firm has been rumored to be linked to organized crime. Susan Shire's TV show is in danger of being canceled next season. Oh, and Barry Batten is superstitious. Now, *that's* news!"

Frank laughed. "Come on, let's turn in," he suggested. "Tomorrow is another day."

The phone rang the next morning at eight, just as Frank and Joe were finishing breakfast. Frank answered. It was Barry.

"Gerald made me promise to talk to you guys as soon as possible," he said. "I've got a theory about the jinx."

"We'll be there in twenty minutes," Frank replied. "Half an hour, outside."

Barry said, "Okay, listen, I'm about to go for a swim. Meet me at the pool."

The Waterside Inn swimming pool was off to one side of the main building, enclosed by a fence and a thick hedge. Barry was just coming out when Frank and Joe arrived. He was wearing a thick terrycloth robe and rubbing his head with a towel.

"I've been doing a lot of thinking," he said, when he saw the Hardys. "You can believe me or not, I don't much care. But there really is a jinx. The only thing I haven't figured out yet is whether it's aimed at the meet or at me."

"It wasn't your boat that caught fire yesterday," Frank pointed out. "And you did win the time trials."

"Yeah," Barry replied. "But all that may just be a way to put me off my guard."

Frank looked over at Joe and rolled his eyes. Champion racer or not, this guy seemed to be playing with less than a full deck.

"Hey, what—!" Barry said. He was gazing up at the inn. "My window's open. I know I left it shut."

"Maybe you're looking at the wrong window," Joe suggested. "It's easy to make that mistake."

Barry said, "I'm in the corner room, right over the veranda roof. And the window's open!"

He broke into a run. Frank and Joe followed him into the inn and up the stairs. His door was at the end of the corridor. Barry fumbled with his key, pushed the door open, and rushed into the room. After turning a full 360 degrees, his eyes came to rest on the dresser.

"It's gone!" he shouted. "My lucky charm—it's gone. Somebody stole it. I *knew* this meet was jinxed!"

11 Barry Breaks Down

"Let's take it easy," Frank said, scanning the room. "Maybe you forgot where you put the medallion."

"Or maybe it fell behind the furniture," Joe suggested.

Barry's square jaw jutted out as he gave Joe a dirty look. "What kind of idiot do you think I am?" he demanded. "I know perfectly well where I left it—right here on top of the dresser. And I know I left the window closed. Some rat sneaked in here and stole my lucky medallion, you hear? And I know who it was, too. That eco-nut who threatened me yesterday, her or her little buddy."

Wordlessly, Joe went over to the dresser and peered behind it, then got down on his hands and knees to scan the floor under it and under the bed. Barry watched, scowling. When Joe stood up empty-handed, he said, "What did I tell you, wise guy?"

Frank went to the door and glanced into the corridor. Several curious faces looked back at him from other doorways. Obviously, Barry's voice had carried. Frank quietly closed the door and turned back to Barry.

"How long were you away from the room?" he asked.

Barry looked confused. "Uh . . . half an hour? Maybe a little more? I went down to the pool right after I called you guys."

"That was at eight," Frank said, mostly to himself. "And we met you at the pool just after eight-thirty. So the room was empty for about half an hour. If someone were watching for you to leave, he or she would have had plenty of time to come in, find the medallion, and split."

"Frank?" Joe called. He was standing next to the open window.

Frank went over to join him. The windowsill and frame were white and recently painted. From the sill, there was a three-foot drop to the mossy shingles of the veranda roof. Frank looked over the sill and the roof, then stooped down to look at them with the light at a different angle. As he straightened up, he met Joe's eyes.

"*Nada*, right?" Joe murmured. "No footprints,

no hand marks, no scratches or smudges. If our burglar came in this way, he managed to do it without touching the roof or the windowsill."

"Maybe it was Peter Pan and he flew in," Frank suggested to Joe, low enough so that Barry couldn't hear. He leaned his head out and craned his neck to look upward. "No sign of anyone forcing the latch, either."

"What are you guys saying?" Barry demanded.

Frank said, "We were just wondering how someone got in through the window without leaving any traces."

"It must have been an experienced burglar," Barry muttered.

"Are you positive that the window and door were locked?" Joe asked.

"What kind of idiot do you think I am?" Barry demanded for a second time. Frank was tempted to tell him, but managed to hold his tongue.

Barry continued, "Of course they were locked. Some detectives you turned out to be!"

Frank froze. Then he looked over at Joe, who seemed as taken aback as he was. "Detectives?" Frank said in a mild voice. "Where'd you get that from, Barry?"

Barry stared at him. "From Gerald, of course," he replied. "Why do you think I asked you to come talk to me?"

"When did he tell you?" Joe demanded.

"Why—last night, after dinner," Barry said. "I

was telling him how worried I am about all this stuff that's been happening. That's when he told me about you guys. He said you had the situation under control. Under control . . . ha!"

"Who else was around when he told you this?" Frank asked.

Barry shrugged. "I didn't notice. Anyway, who cares? That's not going to get my medallion back, is it?"

Frank returned to the door and studied it. It had a spring latch that locked automatically when the door shut, and a dead bolt as well. He pulled the door open and looked closely at the lock. There was no sign of recent scratching. He shut the door and turned to face Barry. "I don't think there's much more we can do here at this point," Frank said.

"I didn't notice you doing much of anything," Barry said, almost smugly. "I'm not surprised."

Frank saw Joe open his mouth to make an angry reply. He touched Joe on the arm, as a signal for him to hold it in. Joe scowled, but he didn't say anything.

"We'll let you know if we have any more questions," Frank said coolly.

Barry gave a snort of derision. "I don't need any more questions," he declared. "Just some answers—and you guys seem fresh out of those."

Frank rolled his eyes, then gestured with his head for Joe to follow him out of the room. As they walked toward the stairs, Joe said, "What a dork! I wouldn't be surprised if he hid the medallion himself."

"Why would he do that?" asked Frank.

"No idea," Joe replied. "To get publicity? Or just because he's such a dork?"

"Poor Dave," Frank said. "He actually got a chance to race, and now this. . . ."

They reached the foot of the stairs just as Gerald Magnusson came rushing up. The dozen or more competitors who were standing around the lobby, talking among themselves, followed him over. Frank spotted Dennis, Susan, and Carl among them.

"What's this I hear?" Gerald demanded. "Was Barry's lucky piece really stolen?"

Frank said carefully, "It does seem to be missing. He thinks someone sneaked in the window of his room while he was at the pool."

"Terrible!" Gerald exclaimed. "We all know how much that charm means to Barry. He must be devastated."

Dennis stepped forward. Thoughtfully stroking his beard, he said, "Gerald, this has to stop. First, all these so-called accidents, and now this. What's the committee going to do about it?"

"Dennis, we're all just as concerned as you are," Gerald said smoothly. "If some misguided person or group is trying to disrupt our meet, we intend to make sure they don't succeed."

102

He turned and motioned toward Frank and Joe. "Some of you have already met Frank and Joe Hardy," he continued. "What you don't know is that their father is the famous investigator Fenton Hardy."

Frank managed to keep the shock he felt from showing on his face. Had Magnusson forgotten that he and Joe were supposed to be working undercover? And if Magnusson decided that keeping them anonymous had lost its usefulness, couldn't he at least have warned them before making a public announcement?

Magnusson continued, "Joe and Frank themselves have a fast growing reputation as detectives. At my request, they've agreed to look into the situation here. I'm one hundred percent sure they have the situation under control. Boys, is there anything you'd like to say at this point?"

Frank thought quickly. Clearing his throat, he said, "Well, we can't really say anything about the leads we've developed so far. But if any of you have noticed anything unusual, I hope you'll let us know." Frank gave the group the number of his home and car phone, and added, "Any calls will be kept confidential. Joe?"

"That about covers it, I guess," Joe said. "If all of us keep our eyes open and our guards up, we'll make it a lot harder for the bad guys to pull anything. Thanks."

The moment Joe finished speaking, about half

the crowd moved in on him and Frank, asking questions and offering suggestions. A similar group clustered around Gerald. No question, the racers were worried.

After fielding comments for a few minutes, Frank raised his voice to say, "I'm sorry, but you'll have to excuse us. We're late for an urgent appointment." He took Joe's elbow and they nudged their way through the crowd and out the front door.

At the sidewalk, Joe paused to ask, "Urgent appointment? With whom?"

"With Connie," Frank replied. "I know she wouldn't talk to us yesterday. But now the situation's changed. She's a suspect, and she could find herself in big trouble. Let's hope she's sensible enough to realize that."

"How do we find her to talk to?" Joe asked.

Frank thought for a moment. "I bet Callie would know where she lives," he said. Callie Shaw was Frank's longtime girlfriend. "She's been involved in a lot of environmental activities."

Frank called Callie from the van and explained what he needed.

"I don't know her number," Callie told him. "But I know she lives over near Sunset Park. Let's see, Fernandez . . . yes, here we are, 4230 Sunset Lane, 555-1939. What do you want with Connie?"

"I'll tell you all about it the next time I see you," Frank promised. "Thanks for the help."

Joe put the van in motion. Frank dialed Connie's number. When she heard who was calling, she almost hung up. "Look, Connie," Frank said quickly. "It's looking worse and worse for you and Earthquest. Joe and I are not out to pin anything on you. We're just trying to find out the truth. And if you haven't done anything wrong, you're going to need help making people believe that. So you really should talk to us."

After a long pause, Connie said, "I'll give you ten minutes."

"We'll be right over," Frank replied.

At Connie's house, they found her waiting in the front yard. She led them around to the back, to a room over the garage. It was furnished with a battered desk and half a dozen metal folding chairs. A color poster on the wall showed a stretch of seashore, with a big drainpipe pouring ugly-looking chemical waste into the water.

"You heard about the fire on Dennis Shire's boat yesterday?" Frank asked, after they'd sat down. Connie nodded, wide-eyed.

Joe said, "We have a witness who saw you hanging around there before it happened."

Connie took a deep breath. "I can explain that," she said. It sounded to Frank as if she had been expecting the question. "My grandfather is

105

Mexican-American, and his favorite song is called 'Adelita.' It's an old folk song. So when I saw the name on that boat, it got my attention. But I never set foot on the boat. All I did was stand there, thinking of my grandfather. Then this big thug from Newcastle Trucking came and chased me away."

"A guy in a green uniform?" Frank asked. She nodded. "Yeah, he hassled us, too. Where were you between eight and eight-thirty this morning?"

"Right here," Connie replied, with a new tone of alarm in her voice. "Why? What's it to you?"

"It looks like somebody sneaked into Barry Batten's room and took his medallion," Joe said.

For a long moment, Connie stared silently into space. Then she shook herself and said, "Well, it wasn't me. Just the idea of touching something carved out of whale ivory makes me sick to my stomach. And I haven't been away from the house all morning. My mom can vouch for that."

"What about Angelo?" Joe asked.

Connie jumped to her feet. "That's it! Angelo was right, you're just trying to discredit our organization. Get out of here, right now!"

Frank blinked in surprise. Why had Connie just exploded like that? "Now, wait," he began.

"No, get out!" Connie repeated, her voice rising. "Before I scream for help!"

"Okay, okay," Joe said, getting up from his chair. "We're out of here."

Before leaving, Frank tore a sheet from his notebook and scribbled their phone numbers on it. "If you change your mind, get in touch," he said.

As they drove off, Frank said, "Did you notice that she didn't really get upset until we asked about Angelo? I wonder if he's the one who's up to something, and she knows it."

Joe's reply was cut short by the buzz of the cellular phone. Frank picked it up.

"Listen," a muffled voice said. "I just spotted somebody messing with the race buoys. If you hurry, you can catch him red-handed."

"Who is this?" Frank demanded. The only response was a click. He told Joe what the caller had said.

"Sounds a little fishy," Joe said, speeding up. "But what'll it cost us to check it out?"

"Go for it," Frank said.

Joe parked in the Waterside Inn lot. He and Frank dashed across the street to the marina and sprinted to the slip where *Sleuth* was tied up. Frank took the helm, while Joe cast off the lines.

Once the boat was clear of the slip, Frank pushed the throttle forward and steered for the harbor mouth. A couple of hundred yards ahead, a group of windsurfers was crossing his course. The brightly colored sails shone against the blue sky and water.

Frank started to pull the throttle back, to slow

107

down before passing the windsurfers. Suddenly he let out a startled exclamation.

"What is it?" Joe demanded. "What's wrong?"

"The throttle!" Frank replied. He wiggled the lever back and forth. It moved much too freely. "It's not responding!"

The rising whine of the powerful outboard covered Joe's reply. Frank stared, horrified. The windsurfers were now dead ahead and Frank could not slow down!

12 Throttle Down!

"Frank, look out!" Joe shouted. "Slow down!"

By now the group of windsurfers was less than fifty yards away. Some of them, alerted by the roar of *Sleuth*'s motor, looked around to see where it was coming from. One surfer, in a green and black wetsuit, was so startled that he lost his balance and fell backward into the water.

"I can't slow down," Frank shouted back. "The cable must be broken. Kill the engine, quick!"

Joe instantly understood. He stood up and lunged back toward the stern of the boat. But just at that moment, Frank put the wheel hard over to port, to avoid the windsurfers. The boat banked sharply. Joe lost his balance and went sprawling to the deck. His head slammed into the siderail.

For one moment Joe imagined that he was on the football field. Someone on defense had just blindsided him. Then he remembered where he was and what he had to do. He shook his head to clear it, then crawled over the rear bench seat. The manual throttle on the big outboard was under the engine housing and hidden by a thicket of control cables. Joe groped for it, being careful not to touch the hot metal housing, and gave it a hard twist to the left. The motor coughed and died.

Sleuth settled into the water and began to rock from the effect of its own wake. Joe straightened up and looked around. The windsurfers were now gliding past the starboard beam, near enough for him to see their frightened expressions. Some of them looked angry. That had been close.

Joe rejoined Frank at the helm. "What happened?" he demanded. "Did the throttle cable break?"

Frank looked up at him grimly. "No, it came unscrewed," he replied. "Here, take a look."

He held up the end of the cable. Joe studied it. There were fresh scratches on the locking collar. "Somebody must have loosened it until it was just barely on," he said.

"And when I pushed it to full ahead, it came off," Frank said, finishing the thought. "What would you like to bet that that call about some-

110

body messing with the buoys was a hoax, to lure us out onto the water?"

"Uh-huh. And— Frank, wait," Joe said. He felt a thrill of excitement. "Whoever made that call had to know the number of our cellular phone. That means we can narrow it down to one of the people in the lobby this morning."

"Not quite," Frank said, with a shake of the head. "I gave Connie our numbers, remember?"

The thrill died down. "Oh, right," Joe said. "I forgot. But, hey, that was right before we left her. And the call came through just five minutes or so later. Awfully fast work."

"Fast, yeah, but just barely possible," Frank replied. "If she knew how to contact Angelo, and he was already at the marina, he could have called us, then jiggered the throttle cable. I'm not saying they did it, but we can't cross them off."

It took ten minutes of concentrated work to reattach the throttle cable and motor back to the dock. Joe and Frank jumped out, tied up *Sleuth*, and went straight to the Earthquest slip. The big rubber boat was there. So was Angelo. He had his back to them, as he rummaged through a jumbled wooden locker.

"Angelo?" Frank said. "We need to talk."

Angelo jumped up and whirled around to face the Hardys. He reached out to close the locker door, but Joe put out an arm and stopped him. On the floor of the locker, peeping out from under a

111

pile of orange life preservers, was a compact but powerful bolt cutter—the exact tool that could have been used to sever the cables on the marker buoys.

"What do you need that for?" Joe demanded, pointing at the bolt cutter.

Angelo looked down, then used his heel to kick the tool farther out of sight under the life preservers. "None of your business," he said sullenly.

"Somebody messed with our boat this morning," Frank told him. "You wouldn't know anything about it, would you?"

"Not a thing. Get lost," Angelo retorted. He started to turn his back on them. Joe reached out to stop him. But at the first touch of Joe's hand, Angelo spun back around and knocked Joe's arm away.

"Keep your hands off me," he shouted.

Joe took a step back and held up his hands, palms outward. "Okay," he said. "Take it easy."

"Angelo, do you know anything about Barry Batten's medallion?" Frank asked.

Angelo scowled at him. "I know somebody ought to rip it off his neck and throw it back in the ocean where it belongs," he replied.

"Somebody took it from his room this morning," Joe said.

"Great!" Angelo said. "But if you clowns think you can pin it on me, you can take a long hike on a short pier." He turned and walked away.

"We're wasting our time with this guy," Frank muttered, turning his back to Angelo. "Let's go back to the inn. I'd like to find out if anybody saw him hanging around there earlier today."

They left the marina and made their way through the crowds to the inn. As they started up the walk, Joe noticed that a painter had set up her easel on the hill overlooking the inn and the harbor. How long had she been there?

"I'll be right back," Joe murmured to Frank. He crossed the lawn and climbed the slope in long, impatient strides.

The painter was in her twenties, wearing a wide-brimmed straw hat and a light-colored, paint-stained smock. She gave Joe a cautious glance as he approached, then concentrated on her canvas. Joe looked over her shoulder. The bright colors were applied in wide, strong brush strokes, but he could recognize the harbor, the crowds, and the corner of the inn veranda.

"Er, excuse me," Joe said. "I'm sorry to bother you, but have you been up here for long?"

She glanced over her shoulder. "Why do you ask?" she replied.

"There was a burglary at the inn this morning," Joe explained. "Supposedly, the crook got into the room from the veranda roof. Since you've got a good view of it from up here . . ."

The painter frowned in concentration. "I got here about eight," she said at last. "And I've been here all the time since then. I'm sure I would have noticed if anybody had climbed on the porch roof, and I didn't see anybody."

"Thanks," Joe said. "That's a big help."

He dashed down the slope to rejoin Frank and quickly explained what he had learned.

"Just as we thought," Frank said, nodding. "It was an inside job. The open window was to make us believe that the burglar came from outside."

Joe had a sudden thought. "Could Barry have done it himself? Hidden the medallion, then arranged for us to find out about the theft?"

"Of course he could have," Frank replied. "Nothing easier. But why?"

"Uh . . . I have no idea," Joe admitted.

"When we went upstairs with him and he unlocked his door, how many times did he turn the key?" Frank asked.

Joe stared off toward the water as he tried to recall. "Hmm . . . I think he just put it in and gave it a half turn. I don't remember hearing a click."

"That's what I thought, too," Frank said. "Which means that he didn't have the dead bolt on, just the spring latch. Come on—I'd like another look at that door."

As they entered the lobby, Joe noticed a crowd clustered around the television set in the far corner of the room. He nudged Frank, and they went over to find out what was going on.

On the screen, Barry was being interviewed by

114

Peter Singer, the cohost of "Sporting America." Barry's boat and Bayport harbor were in the background. Singer was asking, "What does this loss mean to you, Barry?"

"It means I'm finished with powerboat racing," Barry replied.

The gasps from the watchers covered his next few words.

". . . my ancestor's medallion," Joe heard. "It's not that I'm superstitious. It's a question of family pride and family tradition. When I wore that medallion in a race, I felt I stood for something more than myself. Without it . . . well, it just wouldn't be the same, that's all."

"Do the police have any leads?" the interviewer asked.

Barry shrugged. "I haven't been to the police," he said. "And as long as I get my medallion back, I'm not planning to press charges. Maybe this is just a very bad joke somebody played on me. I hope so."

Dave was in front of Frank. Frank tapped him on the shoulder and whispered, "Is this live?"

Dave looked at him blankly. Joe realized that he must be in shock, watching his big break going down the drain. When Frank repeated his question, Dave shook his head as if to clear it, then said, "Yeah, I guess so. I don't know."

He turned back to watch the interview. Frank took Joe's elbow and urged him toward the stairs.

115

When they reached the second floor, Frank said in an undertone, "Barry's room should be empty. Let's try that door."

They hurried to the end of the corridor, and Frank rapped softly on the door, then listened intently. "Not a peep," he reported. He reached for his wallet and took out a gas company credit card. Inserting it into the crack between the door and the jamb, he slowly slid it upward until it hit the latch. Joe stopped watching at that point and scanned the corridor. After a long, agonizing moment, he heard a faint click. He turned, just as Frank, grinning, pushed the door open.

"So much for security," Frank murmured, as he pulled the door closed again. "Anybody who had access to the inn could have taken the medallion."

Joe said, "We've been working on the idea that somebody is trying to wreck the races. But what if Barry was the real target all along? He was the favorite to win, after all. Maybe one of the other racers decided to improve his or her chances by getting Barry out of the race."

"They couldn't know that he'd drop out like that," Frank pointed out. "But it was a cinch that losing his lucky charm would upset him. Maybe you've got a point, Joe. Let's check our answering machine. Maybe somebody's phoned in a tip."

They walked out to the van. Joe dialed their home phone and waited for the machine to pick up. Then he punched in the access code and playback command. Frank passed him a pad and pen.

"Only one message," Joe reported, a couple of minutes later. "It was from Claude, Dad's friend in Vegas. He wants us to call back."

"Hmm . . . that's a pretty sensitive business," Frank said. "I'd rather not call him from the cellular phone, in case someone eavesdrops. Let's go by the house to call him back."

"Okay," Joe replied. "But don't expect me to find such a choice spot to park when we come back."

He reached for the ignition key and turned it. But instead of the sound of the starter motor, he heard a long, high-pitched whistle. Joe knew instinctively that that was the sound of something deadly coming from under the hood.

13 A Booming Case

For one second Joe was too astonished to react. Then he grabbed the door handle, flung the door open, and leaped out. He hit the ground running. The muffled explosion came just as he threw himself to the pavement behind the car in the next slot.

He pushed himself to his hands and knees and looked around. Frank was sprawled on the grass a dozen feet away. He looked dazed but okay. The van seemed okay, too, except for the dense white smoke billowing out from the engine compartment.

Joe stood up. Frank was on his feet now, too, bending over to brush the grass off his jeans. He looked furious.

"Are you all right?" Frank asked.

"I banged my elbow, jumping out of the van," Joe reported. "Other than that, I'm fine. But I'd like to know the name of the joker who wired that firework to our ignition. I'd like a few minutes alone with him, too."

"I've got dibs on him after you," Frank said. He went around to the driver's side door, reached in, and pulled the hood release. He lifted the hood, then backed away and turned his head to avoid the fumes. It smelled like the Fourth of July.

Joe, next to him, pointed toward the distributor. "There it is," he said.

Wires led from the distributor to a red cardboard tube about six inches long. The black letters on the side read Screamin' Meemie—Harmless Thrills.

"Right, I'm thrilled," Frank remarked. "But look at it this way. It could just as easily have been a real bomb. Somebody wanted to send us a message."

"Yeah, and it reads 'butt out,'" Joe said. "No signature, though. Well, I'd better see about getting rid of this gizmo."

While Joe went to get the tool kit, Frank straightened up and looked around. On the other side of the parking lot, a groundskeeper had stopped his riding mower to stare. Frank walked over to him and said, "Hi there."

The groundskeeper nodded and said, "Your van

119

okay? For a minute there, I thought it was a real bomb. Some people have a pretty strange sense of humor."

"I don't think there's any damage," Frank told him. "I wouldn't mind knowing who did it, though. You didn't notice anyone hanging around there, did you?"

The man scratched his bristly chin. "Not exactly, not to recognize," he replied slowly. "But I did notice a tow truck double-parked right in front of your van. That was about an hour ago. I figured somebody had car trouble, but then the truck pulled out without anybody in tow."

"Did you get a look at the driver?" Frank asked eagerly. "You didn't see him fiddling with the hood of the van, did you?"

"Nope. The truck blocked my view," the groundskeeper told him.

"How about the truck itself?" Frank continued. "Did you notice a company name on it?"

The man shook his head. "Sorry, no. Must have been private. It was dark green, if that's any help."

Newcastle! Frank realized with a jolt. His boat was dark green, and so were his employees' uniforms. It would have to be checked, but Frank was ready to bet that the tow trucks for Newcastle's trucking company were dark green, too. He felt his jaw tighten, as he remembered the run-in he and Joe had had with Newcastle's mechanic, Skip. Had Skip put the firework in the van as a way of getting back at the Hardys? Or was there more to it than that? This clearly called for a conference.

"Thanks," Frank said, and hurried back to tell Joe what he had learned.

Joe saw the possibilities as quickly as Frank had. "How's this?" Joe said. "Newcastle's the one I heard making that big bet last night on the phone. But he wants to make absolutely sure he wins. So this guy Skip has been doing a number on some of the other boats. He's the one who jiggered the oil seal on Barry's boat the other day and loosened the fuel line on *Adelita*."

"And since he's Newcastle's mechanic," Frank pointed out, "he not only knows what he's doing, he has a perfect excuse to be out on the dock at all hours. All he needed to do was watch for the right moment. It makes sense, Joe."

Frank paused for a moment to sort out his thoughts, then added, "Then, this morning, Gerald told everybody that we're detectives. Newcastle suddenly realized that we're not just a couple of guys hanging around, that we're actively trying to unmask the saboteur . . . *his* saboteur."

"Yeah, and the next thing we know, somebody's messed with the throttle cable on *Sleuth* and wired a firecracker to the engine of our van," Joe said. "Those are both pretty technical jobs, too. It all adds up, Frank, it really does. The question is, how do we prove it?"

"I don't know if we can," Frank admitted. "But

121

we can try to build a case. We already have one witness who can place Skip at *Adelita* during the most likely time for the sabotage to the fuel line— Connie. And we've got a witness who saw a dark green tow truck next to our van. Now we need to find out if Skip drives a truck like that."

"If he does, we can try to find out if he was in a position to pull off those other nasty tricks," Joe pursued. "Even if we don't succeed, if we ask enough questions, we might make him and his buddies so nervous that they make a mistake and give themselves away."

"Uh-oh, we're forgetting something," Frank said, glancing at his wrist. "The elimination heats begin in just over an hour. Any witness we might want to talk to is going to be out on the water, watching the races."

"Hey, bro, *I* want to be out there, too!" Joe retorted. "We'd better hurry up and solve this case, so we can enjoy the regatta. What about that call to Claude? We can't get back in time if we go home now."

Frank thought for a moment. "If we use a pay phone, I can't imagine that the bad guys will have a tap on it. Let's chance it."

They walked along Shore Road to the phone on the corner of Water Street. While Joe scanned the area for possible listeners, Frank put through the call to Las Vegas.

"Hey, you had it on the nose," Claude said,

after Frank identified himself. "The last couple of days have seen some very heavy action on that boat race you asked me about."

"Let me guess," Frank said. "Somebody's been betting a lot of money that Carl Newcastle will win. Am I right?"

Claude chuckled. "You've been reading yesterday's paper, good buddy. That's when most of the betting was on Newcastle. Today the heavy hitters are swinging for Batten."

"What?" Frank stared at the phone in astonishment. "But he practically pulled out of the race this morning. It was on national TV."

"I know, I saw it," Claude replied. "So did the oddsmakers. Yesterday, he was the clear one-to-four favorite. That means if you bet a buck on him and he won, the bookie would pay you one dollar. But if he lost, you'd owe the bookie four bucks. After that broadcast, though, you'd stand to win two dollars for every dollar you bet . . . if he runs and wins."

Frank asked, "What happens if you bet on somebody who *doesn't* stay in the race?"

"In that case, you are fresh out of luck, my friend," Claude replied. "It makes you wonder why somebody would put thousands of smackers on a guy who just told the world he's splitsville. If you find out the answer, let me know."

Frank thanked Claude for his help and hung up. He told Joe what he had learned.

"That doesn't make any sense at all," Joe said. "Maybe somebody saw that the odds had changed but didn't realize why."

"One of those 'suckers born every minute,' you mean?" Frank replied. "Could be. In any case, we did confirm that somebody put a lot of money on Newcastle, so that part of our theory still holds. Let's get over to the marina and see if we can find anyone who saw Skip hanging around someplace he shouldn't have been."

"Sure thing," Joe said. "But don't forget, we've got to get a move on if we're going to grab a good spot to watch the races."

"No way I'd forget that," Frank assured his brother. "Come on!"

An hour later *Sleuth* was anchored just off the buoy-marked channel, about eight miles from Bayport harbor. It was one of a long row of boats loaded with spectators.

"Too bad there's no scoreboard," Joe said, after the last of the two dozen boats roared past. It was the first lap of the first elimination race. "It's great to see them run, but it'd be even greater if we knew who won."

"That was Susan's boat in the lead," Frank said. "I didn't see *Adelita* or Newcastle's boat, though. I guess they'll be running in the second race."

"Here come the others," Joe said. He grabbed

124

the binoculars and focused them on the speeding boats. "Susan's still got the lead, but there's a red boat that's really pushing her. Number D-103. It's going wide to pass. . . ."

Frank choked off an exclamation. The red boat must have hit Susan's wake at a bad angle. The bow, already elevated by the boat's speed, rose higher and higher. It looked as if the boat had decided to turn itself into a rocket. Then the force of the wind caught the hull like a giant sail. In an instant, the boat flipped over.

"We've got to do something!" Joe shouted. "Start the engine! I'll pull the anchor."

Frank grabbed his arm. "No, let the marshals handle it," he said quickly. "If a bunch of civilians like us run straight into the path of the racers, we'll have a *real* disaster."

Within minutes the driver and throttleman had been taken on board a marshal's boat and their damaged boat was being towed away. And a few minutes after that, the racers came screaming by on their second lap. Frank noticed that the line was a lot thinner and more stretched out.

"Dave wasn't kidding when he told us how tough this is on the boats," he remarked. "Barry's really lucky that he won the time trials and doesn't have to race today. Now that I've seen what these boats go through, I'm surprised any of them make it to the finish line."

125

"I just hope Dennis and Miguel do all right," Joe replied. "Who knows what kind of hidden damage that fire might have done to the engines."

"We'll know soon enough," Frank said.

There was a long intermission after the first heat. Joe hailed a passing check boat and found out that Susan had come in first in Open Class. The other three big boats hadn't even finished.

"I guess that means tomorrow's field is down to five boats," Frank said when he heard this. "Barry, Susan, the first two in the next heat, and the winner of the consolation heat."

"And if Newcastle's one of them, and Barry really does pull out . . ." Joe replied.

"Then Newcastle will have just three rivals to deal with," Frank said, finishing the thought. "If you ask me, they're going to need protection."

Finally the second heat started. When the pack came into sight, *Adelita* was several lengths ahead of Newcastle's dark green boat. Dennis kept his lead on the return leg and throughout the second lap. Frank found himself crossing his fingers and hoping that nothing broke.

Maybe the spell worked. On the last lap, the two lead boats still held the same positions, roaring down the return leg at what looked like easily 120 miles per hour. Frank didn't see the other two Open Class competitors at all.

"Do you want to stay and watch the consolation

126

heat?" Joe asked. "Or should we get back to work?"

Frank grinned at him. "This *was* work," he retorted. "Even if it was fun at the same time. But I guess we'd better go in."

The return to Bayport was slow, because there were so many boats out on the water. The harbor itself, and the marina, were practically deserted. Finally, Frank nosed *Sleuth* into their slip. Joe took the bowline and stepped up onto the dock. He was slipping the loop over a bollard when Frank saw a hulking figure jump up from behind a storage shed and run at him. He was wearing a mask and held a baseball bat up over his shoulder.

Frank opened his mouth to shout a warning. At that instant, he felt *Sleuth* rock under a sudden weight. He spun around. A second man, in camouflage overalls and a ski mask, was crouched in the stern of the boat. He raised his baseball bat in his right hand and took a menacing step toward Frank.

14 Newcastle Checkmate

Joe sensed a sudden movement out of the corner of his eye and heard the sound of rushing steps. He turned just in time to see a bat hurtling toward his head. He threw himself forward and to the right. The bat hit his shoulder a glancing blow. His left arm went numb and hung useless at his side. He walled off the glaring pain in a far corner of his mind and concentrated on his first priority, fighting and defeating his attacker.

Dropping into a half crouch, Joe charged forward, head down, and butted the other guy in the stomach. The guy let out a *whoosh!* and bent double. Instantly, Joe used his powerful thigh muscles to propel himself upward, slamming the top of his head into his opponent's chin. The

128

masked man reeled back, but recovered. He grabbed Joe's shirtfront and tried to knee him in the face.

Joe dodged to the left and took the force of the guy's knee on his good shoulder. Then he aimed a punch at the side of his opponent's throat. The guy managed to block the attack with his forearm, but to do so, he had to let go of the bat. Joe grabbed it in midair.

"Okay, turkey," Joe growled. "*My* inning!" One-handed, he made a backhand swing in the direction of his attacker's knees. With a yelp of fear, the guy stumbled backward a few steps. Then he turned and ran.

Joe turned, too, but in the other direction, back toward *Sleuth*. Frank was crouched near the stern, grappling with the other masked man. The boat rocked wildly from side to side.

Just as Joe ran down the dock to join the battle, Frank's attacker managed to work his right arm free. He raised his baseball bat, preparing to club Frank across the back of the head. Without thinking, Joe lifted the bat he had wrested from the other thug and threw it, spear fashion. As it left his hand, he had a sudden fear that he would hit Frank. But the bat flew true, hitting Frank's opponent in the ribs, just under his upraised arm. He staggered back. *Sleuth* rocked so far to port that water sloshed in. Off balance, the thug tumbled

129

backward into the water. He kept his hold on Frank's arm, though, dragging him in, too.

Pausing just long enough to slip out of his shoes, Joe made a racing dive into the harbor. When he surfaced and looked around, Frank was treading water a few feet away. His attacker was climbing up onto the dock on the far side of the next slip. The moment he got to his feet, he broke into a run. The battle was obviously over.

"We should take the boat back out," Frank said. "Those goons might be going for reinforcements."

They climbed in and motored out into the bay. "Let's tie up at one of the temporary berths on the other side of the marina," Frank suggested. "No one will expect us there."

Joe scanned the docks as they passed. Then he happened to glance down at the deck. His eyes widened. He bent down and fished something from under the seat.

"Frank! Look at this!" he exclaimed.

Joe was holding a brown leather wallet. He opened it and whistled. "A bunch of brand-new fifty-dollar bills," he reported. "Eight . . . nine . . . ten of them. And a Newcastle Trucking ID card in the name of Ralph Waldvogel, who looks an awful lot like our pal, Skip. Frank, this is the proof we needed against Newcastle! We'd better find Magnusson, fast, and tell him what we know!"

* * *

Gerald Magnusson was at the inn, attending a reception for the racers. When Joe and Frank walked in, both dripping wet, he spotted them at once and hurried over.

"We need to talk, right away," Frank told him.

"All right, let's go to my office," Magnusson replied.

Once in the office, Magnusson listened gravely as the Hardys explained why they thought that Carl Newcastle was behind the sabotage campaign. Then Joe showed him the wallet and told him where he had found it.

"It's hard to believe," Magnusson said, slowly shaking his head. "Oh, you've convinced me. But if someone had told me a week ago that one of our competitors would do such a cowardly thing . . ."

Magnusson picked up the phone and asked the inn desk to page Newcastle. After a short pause, he said, "Carl, may I see you, right away? It's important. Of course I'm sure." He replaced the receiver and sat back with his shoulders squared, looking like someone facing a task he disliked.

"You need to see me?" Newcastle said from the doorway. "What's the problem?"

"Come in and close the door, Carl," Magnusson said. "I've just heard some very disturbing allegations about you."

Newcastle narrowed his eyes and aimed them at Joe and Frank. "What have these kids been saying about me?" he demanded.

Joe stepped forward. "We found out that your mechanic, Skip Waldvogel, and another one of your employees have been pulling dirty tricks on your rivals," he said.

Frank then listed what he believed Newcastle's goons had messed with: the fuel line on the *Adelita*, the throttle cable on the *Sleuth*, the firecracker in the van, the missing buoy. "And we were just attacked by two of your men with baseball bats," Frank continued. "We have proof," he added.

Newcastle didn't ask what proof. After a short silence, he said, "If one of my employees went a little too far in trying to help me win, I'm sorry. But it's got nothing to do with me."

"I'm sorry, Carl. That's not good enough," Magnusson said. "It would be wise for you to withdraw from tomorrow's race . . . a mechanical problem with your boat, perhaps."

"Now, wait a minute," Newcastle said, raising his voice.

Magnusson held up his hand. "The alternative is to bring this whole business before the race committee," he said. "I'd prefer to avoid that kind of publicity, wouldn't you? And there's an excellent chance that you'd be barred from off-shore racing for good. Do you want to take that risk?"

In the tense silence, Joe saw the muscle in

132

Newcastle's jaw start to twitch. Then the trucking executive slammed his hand down on Magnusson's desk. "Okay, I withdraw," he said. "But you and your boy detectives better listen to this. Anybody who says publicly that I did anything crooked had better know a good lawyer . . . and a good doctor!"

He stared at Joe and Frank, as if memorizing their faces. Then he stormed out of the room.

Magnusson took a deep breath and let it out slowly. "Well," he said. "That's that. Frank, Joe— you've earned my congratulations and thanks."

"Actually, the case isn't tied up just yet," Frank said. "We still don't know for certain who sent you the fax of the leaflet. The same goes for the leaflet with the threatening message that we found in Dennis's file. I can't come up with any motive for Newcastle to threaten you or Dennis with the leaflet. Connie could be responsible for that, of course, but we don't know for sure. Plus, we don't know who poisoned Chuck, or if it was intentional at all."

"Don't forget Barry's medallion is still missing," Joe added.

"Right," Frank said. "And there's nothing to tie Newcastle to the theft."

"Ah, yes, the medallion," Magnusson said. "Well, after seeing the splendid detective work you did today, I wouldn't be surprised if you

133

manage to turn up the medallion as well. I'd better get back to the reception. You'll join me, won't you?"

It was dinnertime when Joe and Frank finally left the inn and drove home. Their mother was in the front hallway, on the phone. Joe heard her say, "Oh, they just walked in. Do you want to say hello? Hold on."

She passed the phone to Joe, who was closer. He said hello and heard his father's voice say, "How are you getting along with that boating case?"

"Pretty well, Dad," Joe replied. "I think we've got it close to wrapped up."

"Great," Fenton said. "I'll want to hear all about it when I get home. Oh, give Magnusson a big hello from Steve Griffin."

"Your client?" Joe asked. "They know each other?"

"Oh, sure. They go way back," Fenton replied. "Steve was surprised that Magnusson had tried to get me to take this case you're on. Apparently Steve mentioned to Magnusson just a couple of weeks ago that I was coming out to the West Coast to give him a hand. I guess my name stuck in Magnusson's mind and the facts that went with it didn't. Oops—there's Steve at the door now. Talk to you later."

* * *

134

The next morning Frank was heating the waffle iron and Joe was stirring batter when the phone rang. Frank grabbed it and said hello.

A gruff voice said, "You want to break this case wide open? Keep a close watch on the Fernandez girl."

"Who is this?" Frank demanded. There was silence, then a dial tone.

Frank repeated the message to Joe.

"I think we already saw this show," Joe said. "What now? We rush out to the van, drive off, and find out that somebody cut the brake line?"

Frank grinned. "Nope. We have a nice, hot breakfast. We give the van a nice, thorough check. Then we go park down the street from Connie's house for a nice, peaceful stakeout."

"There goes our morning," Joe grumbled.

Half an hour later, as they circled Connie's block looking for a parking space, Joe was still grumbling. "I'll bet we sit here for an hour or two and nothing happens," he said.

"You lose," Frank replied, sliding down in his seat. "There's Connie backing out now. Don't get close enough for her to spot us."

"Are you trying to teach me how to do my job?" Joe groused. He let Connie get all the way to the corner before he put the van in motion again.

Connie didn't seem to be in a hurry. The slow-motion pursuit led across town to a seedy strip shopping center. Joe parked at the far end of the lot, then he and Frank followed Connie at a distance. She approached a row of shabby offices, most of them vacant. After opening a glass door, Connie walked down a hall, checking the signs on the doors, then stopped and tried the knob of one. The door swung open, and she went inside.

"Come on," Frank said urgently. He broke into a run. Joe was right behind him. They burst through the open doorway and stopped short.

The only furniture in the room was a big, battered cardboard carton. Connie was standing next to it, looking over at the Hardys in alarm. On top of the carton were a few scattered Earthquest leaflets.

Frank was beginning to think that Joe was right, and that their morning stakeout had been a bust. But then he saw something that made him inhale sharply and grab Joe's sleeve—an intricately carved ivory medallion on a gold chain.

15 And They're Off!

"Congratulations," Connie said bitterly. "You caught me red-handed."

"It sure looks that way," Frank said.

Connie tossed her head and said, "Of course it does. You guys are really something, aren't you? You must feel proud of yourselves."

Joe took a step forward. "Now hold on," he said. "Are you trying to say that *we*—"

She raised her voice. "Come off it, Joe Hardy! Of course you set me up. Are you going to try to tell me you just happened to be driving by at the exact same time I came here? Give me a break! By the way, which of you made that phone call? You're good at disguising your voice. I never would have thought it was one of you guys."

137

"We followed you here," Frank said. "We were watching your house because *we* got a phone call this morning telling us to."

"Are you for real?" Connie demanded. "You're asking me to believe that whoever set me up set you up, too?"

"Believe it or not," Joe said. "We got a call this morning. And we *did* find you here with Barry's lucky charm, didn't we?"

A shudder went through Connie. "Will you please get that horrible thing out of my sight?" she pleaded. "It makes me sick just to look at it. If I had to touch it, I think I'd keel over."

Frank wondered if Connie wasn't protesting too much. Did she really have such a strong emotional reaction to a piece of whale ivory that was over a hundred years old? Or was she trying to convince them that she wasn't physically capable of stealing it?

"This *does* smell like a frame," Frank said. "But you've still got a lot of explaining to do. What were you and Angelo doing to that buoy the other day?"

When Connie started to protest, Joe said, "We saw the marks on the cable. And we spotted the bolt cutter in your locker at the marina."

Connie stared down at her hands. In a voice so low that Frank had to lean forward to hear, she said, "We didn't do anything. Angelo was kidding around about how easy it would be to, like, totally mess up the races. But when he actually started to

138

cut that cable, I made him stop. I don't think he really meant to, anyway—just to show me he could. And then you guys nearly ran us down."

"Poor you," Joe said, in an unsympathetic voice.

"Look, what we're trying to do is important," Connie said, thrusting her chin out. "We haven't broken any laws, and nobody can prove we did. We had nothing to do with the missing buoy. Earthquest is committed to keeping the waters safe. For all creatures, including humans."

Frank looked at Joe, who gave a tiny shrug. "Well, whether you or someone in your group took Barry's medallion or not," Frank said, "right now the main thing is to get it back to him. He did say he wouldn't press charges if he got it back."

"I don't care if he does press charges," Connie said. "We're the victims in this, not him."

Joe said, "If you're in jail, you won't be able to spread your message to the public."

Connie's eyes widened. "Oh, no!" she exclaimed. "Angelo! I said I'd pick him up at nine-thirty. We're going to be leafleting all day. I'd better run."

"We're going, too," Frank said. He reached over and scooped up the medallion. Then he and Joe accompanied Connie out to the parking lot.

"What now—follow her?" Joe asked under his breath.

Frank shook his head. "If we need her, we'll

139

find her easily enough," he said. "Let's get over to the inn. I wonder . . . once he has his medallion back, will Barry decide to race after all?"

The door to Magnusson's office was ajar. Frank tapped on it, then put his head in. Magnusson was on the phone. When he saw Frank and Joe, he motioned for them to come in. Then he held up five fingers to show that he'd be with them in a few minutes.

Frank took a pen and memo pad from Magnusson's desk and wrote, "We found the medallion." He tore off the page and held it up for Magnusson to read. Magnusson's eyes widened. He muttered an excuse to the person on the other end of the phone and hung up. To Joe and Frank, he said, "You really have it? Amazing! I'd better let Barry know, right away."

Magnusson called Barry's room. Frank glanced around for a wastebasket. He didn't see one, so he folded the memo page and stuck it in his shirt pocket. Just then Barry came rushing in.

"Is it true?" he demanded. Frank showed him the medallion. Barry grabbed it and put it around his neck, saying, "Now I'll show those jerks a thing or two. You know what my boat's called?"

Joe said, *"It's Mine*, right?"

"That's right," Barry replied. His mouth twisted into a sneer. "And today's prize cup? And the championship title? Guess what? *It's Mine.*"

He turned and hurried away.

"Thanks a lot for finding my lost lucky piece for me, guys," Joe muttered.

Frank rolled his eyes. "Look, at least this means that Dave will get his big break after all," he said.

"Boys, I'm really proud of you," Magnusson said. "How would you like to watch today's race from the judges' boat? We sail at eleven-thirty sharp. There'll be lunch while we wait for the starting gun."

"We'd love to," Frank said, in the same instant that Joe breathed, "Awesome!"

"Fine. I'll see you then." Magnusson reached for the phone.

As Frank and Joe were leaving the inn, Dennis stopped them. "I hear you guys tracked down Barry's charm," he said. "Lucky for him—it's the closest thing to charm that he has. But couldn't you have waited a few hours? You know, until after the race?" He laughed. "Who took it, anyway?"

"That's not clear," Frank answered.

"Oh?" Dennis raised his eyebrows. "Well, I guess it doesn't really matter, anyway. Even with Barry back in the race, I'm bound to take at least fourth place in Open Class."

"How many are racing?" Joe asked.

Dennis grinned. "In Open? Four—Barry, Susan, Pete Carnofsky, and me. Newcastle pulled out. Hey, who knows? I might even pull down

141

third or second place! But I'd better go make sure Pavel is talking nice to the engines."

The judges' boat was a yacht big enough to make *Sleuth* look like a dinghy. During lunch, in the teak-paneled saloon, Joe and Frank got to know a young man named Sean. He was one of the official timekeepers. Just before the race started, he took them up to the flying bridge to show off his electronic gear.

Joe looked over the notebook computer and the array of digital timers. "This sure beats a stop-watch and a clipboard," he remarked.

"Don't laugh," Sean said. "I've timed races that way, too."

Out on the open water, the racing boats were getting into position for the start. Frank asked, "Why are the biggest, most powerful boats in the first row? That doesn't seem fair."

"It spreads out the field and cuts down on dangerous bunching," Sean explained.

A cabin cruiser loaded with spectators strayed across the course, pursued by one of the marshals.

"What if a bystander gets in the way of one of the racers?" Joe asked. "Would the officials stop the race and rerun it?"

Sean shook his head. "The usual rules of the road still hold," he said. "Just because a boat's in a race doesn't give it any special privileges. Hey, you'd better go now. I have to get to work. You'll have a good view from the bow."

Frank and Joe hurried down to the main deck and weaved through the crowd to a spot near the bow. Three helicopters were now hovering over the field of competitors. Two were marked with the logos of rival sports TV channels. The third carried official observers.

The loud-hailer on the bridge of the judges' boat started broadcasting a countdown. At "zero," there was a flash of flame and a puff of white smoke from a small cannon. Whatever sound it made was completely covered by the sudden roar from dozens of race-tuned, supercharged engines. Tightly bunched, the pack accelerated quickly, throwing up a cloud of spray shot through with rainbows. In what seemed like only moments, all the boats were out of sight.

Frank unclenched his fingers from the wooden rail and said, "Wow! Don't you wish we could hitch a ride with one of them?"

"Why not ask Barry?" Joe suggested. "He owes us."

"Ho, ho," Frank replied, making a face. "That guy has the gratitude of a weasel. I'm almost sorry we got his medallion back. And we still don't know who took it."

"I'm ready to cross off Connie," Joe said. "That scene this morning was too obviously a setup. How about Newcastle? Maybe, after we forced him to drop out of the race, he didn't see any reason to hold on to the medallion any longer."

"But why give it back?" Frank replied. "Why not simply lose it overboard? In fact, why would *anyone* risk stealing the medallion, then turn around and give it back? An attack of bad conscience? I doubt it."

Joe scratched his chin and said, "It looks like the crook wanted to make Barry drop out, then decided that he—or she—wanted him to race after all. But what kind of sense does that make?"

"We've got a few minutes before the racers come in sight again," Frank said. "Let's make a list of possible suspects and motives."

As he reached for his ballpoint, Frank felt the crinkle of paper in his shirt pocket. He took it out and recognized the memo sheet from Magnusson's desk. He was about to start writing his list on it when he noticed a faint line of indentations near the top. It looked like writing, and the first characters looked like 702. Wasn't that the area code for Las Vegas?

"Joe!" Frank said urgently. "Look, those marks show what was written on the sheet before this one. See what you make of them."

By holding the sheet at different angles to the sunlight, they deciphered what looked like a Las Vegas phone number, followed by "BB 5:2 100K."

" 'BB'—Barry Batten!" Joe exclaimed.

"And five to two must be the odds," Frank added. "In other words, someone was planning to bet 100K—a hundred thousand dollars—on Barry, at odds that would pay off a quarter of a million bucks."

"Really?" Joe asked. "Are you sure?"

"One hundred percent sure," Frank replied.

Joe's jaw dropped. "Frank! That's what *he* said—the guy I overheard on the phone at Magnusson's dinner party. And he was checking on BB."

"Magnusson! I'm one hundred percent sure that's where I picked up that phrase. He says it all the time. Joe, that's it!" Frank exclaimed. "I see it now. Magnusson took the medallion, so that Barry would drop out and the odds on him would change. Then he placed his big bet. After that, he arranged for us to find the medallion, so that Barry would race after all. It was all a scheme to manipulate the odds."

"So that's why he asked Dad to take the case, when he already knew Dad was going to be busy in California," Joe said. "Because he knew he'd get us instead."

Frank nodded. "He needed to be able to show that he was doing something about the sabotage, but he didn't want anyone around who'd do *too* good a job. I bet he expected to lead a couple of teenage detectives around by the nose!"

"I guess we surprised him," Joe said. "And all

that business about Earthquest was just a smoke screen. He must have sent himself that fax, and he probably put the other leaflet in Dennis's file. Magnusson then set the scene for us to find the medallion this morning. He wanted us off on a wild-goose chase. Okay, what now?"

"We tell him what we know," Frank replied. "After that . . . well, we'll see."

Joe grabbed his arm. "Look, here come the leaders on the return leg. Barry's in front, but Dennis isn't that far back. Do you think he has a chance to win?"

"With more than two laps still to go?" Frank said. "Anything can happen. Come on."

They found Gerald Magnusson near the stern, next to the gangway. He was leaning over the rail, talking to a man in a speedy-looking runabout. He looked up as the Hardys approached. Something in their faces must have tipped him off.

"Is anything the matter?" he asked warily.

"We have the number of your bookmaker in Vegas," Frank announced. "How do you think he'll react when we tell him how you rigged the odds on today's race?"

"Even if Barry does win," Joe added, "I don't think you're going to collect on your bets. Sorry about that."

"I don't know what you're talking about," Magnusson blustered. "I have more important things to do than listen to this nonsense."

146

He pushed past Frank. Suddenly he turned, jumped down into the idling speedboat, and shoved its occupant over the side, into the water. Joe lunged toward the rail, ready to leap after him, but Frank grabbed his arm and held him back.

"No!" Frank exclaimed. "Too late! Let him go. He can't escape. Besides, by trying to run away, he's just proving that we were right about him."

The speedboat surged forward as Magnusson shoved the throttle to full speed ahead. For a moment, he seemed about to steer for the harbor. But his path was blocked by the hordes of spectator boats. He swung the speedboat to starboard, toward open water . . . and the marked-off channel of the race course.

"No, stop!" Frank shouted, as he suddenly saw the danger. But there was no chance that Magnusson would hear him. Even the loud whine of the speedboat's motor was drowned out by the clamor of the unmuffled thousand-horsepower racers, roaring toward the end of the first lap at well over a hundred miles an hour.

It's Mine, in the lead, was on a collision course with the little speedboat. Barry seemed to see the danger at the same instant as Magnusson. Following deeply ingrained rules of the road, both swerved to starboard. Magnusson's boat, caught in the ferocious wake thrown up by *It's Mine*, flipped over, pitching Magnusson like a rag doll into the water.

147

"He never had a chance of getting away," Joe said, watching a rescue boat take off toward Magnusson.

"I hope he didn't ruin the racers' chances by getting in the way," Frank said, his eyes intent on the racing boats.

Just then Barry and Dave made an S-turn to regain the channel. As they pulled back on the course, Dennis and Miguel roared past, into the lead.

"Nothing can stop those guys," Joe observed. "It's full throttle forward with an eye on the prize."

"So it was Carl's sabotage that gave Gerald the idea?" Dennis asked. He, Miguel, and Dave were sitting with Joe and Frank on the veranda of the Waterside Inn. Dennis still wore the wreath that had been placed around his neck after winning the big race.

"It was a convenient smoke screen," Frank said. "With all the confusion, who would question a stolen lucky charm? Magnusson just had to be sure we got the medallion back to Barry *after* the odds had changed, but in time for the race."

"He's been having business problems," Joe added. "This seemed like a perfect way to get a big wad of quick cash. It nearly worked, too."

"It would have, if not for you," Miguel said. "At the next Powerboat Racing Guild meeting, I'm

148

going to move that you be given life member-
ships."

"I'll second it," Dennis said, smiling. "Dave,
that was a nice job you did, recovering from
Gerald's interference well enough to take second
place. You deserve a better racing partner than
Barry."

Dave grinned. "I've got one—my brother. I
called home after the race, to tell him Barry and I
took second place. He said he thinks he may have
found someone to sponsor a boat for us."

"I hope it works out," Joe said.

"Say, Joe, Frank?" Dennis said. "Are you guys
doing anything three weekends from now? I'm
entered in a race off Cape Cod, and *Adelita*'s got
room for two more."

"We'll be there!" Frank and Joe said, in one
breath.

NANCY DREW® MYSTERY STORIES By Carolyn Keene

A MINSTREL® BOOK

Published by Pocket Books

THE RACE IS ON, AND FRANK AND JOE
ARE ABOUT TO BLOW THE COMPETITION
OUT OF THE WATER!

THE NORTHEAST NATIONAL OFFSHORE RACES
ARE COMING TO BAYPORT, SHOWCASING SOME
OF THE FASTEST AND MOST POWERFUL RACING
BOATS IN THE WORLD. THE WINNER WILL WALK
AWAY WITH A $100,000 PRIZE, BUT MUCH MORE
THAN MONEY IS AT STAKE. SOMEONE IS RIGGING
THE BOATS AND RIGGING THE GAME—PUTTING
EVERY RACER'S LIFE AT RISK!

THE HARDYS ARE NOT ABOUT TO STAND
ONSHORE AND LET DANGER TAKE ITS COURSE.
THEY'RE GOING TO REV UP THEIR ENGINES AND
MAKE SOME WAVES OF THEIR OWN. THE FIX MAY
BE IN, BUT ONCE FRANK AND JOE KICK INTO
GEAR, ALL BETS ARE OFF—BECAUSE WHEN THE
FISTS AND THE FLAMES BEGIN TO FLY, THEY'RE
SURE TO BE RIGHT IN THE THICK OF IT!

A MINSTREL® BOOK
PUBLISHED BY
POCKET BOOKS
RL: 6.2
008-012
PRINTED IN U.S.A.

$3.99 U.S.
$4.99 CAN.

ISBN 0-671-50521-1

5 0 5 2 1 >

UPC

0 76714 00399 6